Cecilia Norman was born in Chelsea, London and studied domestic science. After marriage and raising her two daughters she returned to teaching as a home economics teacher in secondary and further education. For several years she taught Recipe Development and the Preparation of Food for Photography to final year students at both The Polytechnic of North London and Croydon College. She is an expert in all forms of cookery and is the Principal of the Microwave Cooking School in Hampstead. She takes an active interest in the Institute of Home Economics and the British Standards Institution. She has written many books, among which *Pancakes and Pizzas*, *The Pie and Pastry Cookbook* and her *Microwave Cookery Course* are also available in Panther Books.

By the same author

Microwave Cookery for the Housewife
The Heartwatcher's Cook Book
The Colour Book of Microwave Cooking
Freezer to Microwave Cookery
The Crêpe and Pancake Cookbook (re-titled *Pancakes and Pizzas* for paperback)
Microwave Cooking
The Sociable Slimmer's Cookbook
Microwave with Magimix
Microwave Cookery Course
The Pie and Pastry Cook Book

CECILIA NORMAN

Barbecue Cookery

PANTHER
Granada Publishing

Panther Books
Granada Publishing Ltd
8 Grafton Street, London W1X 3LA

First published by Panther Books 1984
Reprinted 1984, 1985

ISBN 0-586-06021-9

Printed and bound in Great Britain by
Cox & Wyman Ltd, Reading

Set in Times

Contents

Acknowledgements	7
Foreword	9
1 – Choosing Your Barbecue	11
2 – Cooking Methods	24
3 – Cooking the Basic Foods	36
4 – Menu Section	44
5 – Grilling	71
6 – Spit Roasting	87
7 – Foil Cookery	95
8 – Frying	107
9 – On Skewers	119
10 – Barbecue Sauces, Marinades and Sundries	131
11 – Dips	141
12 – Savoury Butters	149
13 – Salad Dressings	157
14 – Side Salads	163
15 – Vegetables	175
16 – Soups	187
17 – Desserts	197
18 – Drinks	211
Index	217

Acknowledgements

I would like to thank Alan Davis of Leisureking Ltd for the barbecues; Dilys for her help in working out the recipes; Laurence and Sally for my first barbecue lesson; my husband Laurie who helped me to keep to my deadline; Inmaculada who erected and lit the barbecues nightly throughout the spring and summer; Colin, Kerry and Thomas who ran all the barbecues on the night of the big party when we tested out the recipes on our guests Judge David and Fern Allen of Visalia, California; and lastly but most lovingly Hannah whose milk shake recipe appears in the book.

Foreword

My first experience of a barbecue was in a small town called Visalia in the middle of the Californian desert. The couple that we met quite by chance invited us to a cook-out in their 'back-yard'. It was a still clear night, the temperature somewhere around 100°F; the back-yard was a beautiful well-cared-for garden with short-cut grass and swimming pool. A table was laid with a delicate pink cloth set with immaculate silver cutlery, glistening glasses and, to top it all, a candelabra. The barbecue was an enormous brick-built contraption, and we ate huge T-bone steaks and salads and drank fine Californian wine.

The eating outdoors was great fun but I couldn't imagine us in our London back-yard at near zero temperatures doing the same thing. However, we thought we would give barbecuing a go and in spite of the drawbacks, such as using a battered old garden table and sitting on the backdoor step, we found it a thoroughly enjoyable experience.

Of course we did lots of things wrong, one of them being that we never had the food ready to cook at the right time and the coals burnt out too soon, but it didn't take long to sort out these minor problems and we found barbecuing a great deal of fun, a leisurely pursuit, relaxing and sociable – and somehow the food tasted better.

There are others who like us live in an overcrowded urban area and there are lots of people with gardens who can create a better atmosphere, but whatever your surroundings I hope that this book will be of value to barbecue beginners and that old hands at barbecuing will find some interesting new recipes and ideas.

1

Choosing Your Barbecue

When deciding which barbecue to choose take into consideration how often you are likely to be using it. Bear in mind that you will probably find that you get to like barbecuing and will become addicted – you may even wish to use it in a sheltered spot during the winter. It should be borne in mind that an 'outdoor' barbecue *cannot* be used in the house, although you can cook in the grate if you have a flue with a good draught and sufficient ventilation.

You can either build your own barbecue or you can go out and buy one. To build your own from scratch you will need a base, a grid and some firebricks to go round the sides. An old treadle-sewing-machine base, some old-fashioned fire-backs piled one on top of the other, plus a sturdy wire grid to place on top make a perfectly satisfactory barbecue. It is important to have fire-bricks and not ordinary bricks, although engineering bricks such as Southwater Reds or Staffordshire Blues are excellent. More grandiose barbecues can be constructed up to any size you wish, and at last do-it-yourself barbecue kits are becoming available.

A ready-to-use barbecue does not have to be expensive

DO-IT-YOURSELF

but remember you have to keep it somewhere so buy the size for which you have adequate storage space. You may not wish to dismantle it every time you have finished using it and in any event you can't take it to pieces while it is still hot. Keep the packaging so that you can store away the barbecue each winter.

PICNIC BARBECUES

These fold up like a tool box. A grid inside is adjustable to various heights, although experience has taught me that there is not always enough space to produce sufficient draught to keep the coals going for these are simply placed in the bottom of the box. However, this type is very useful for putting in the boot of a car for a simple cook-out in the country.

PICNIC

HIBACHI BARBECUES

This ever-popular make can be round or rectangular, table top or free standing, of heavy cast iron or made from lighter pressed steel or aluminium. The Hibachi is bulkier than the picnic barbecue and has only a small surface area which limits the amount of food you can cook at any one time, but its advantage is the inclusion of side or front venting which speeds the time taken to ignite and burn through. Choose the deepest type obtainable. Hibachis do not have a cover.

HIBACHI

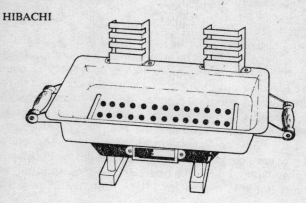

BRAZIER BARBECUES

This type has a collar and a grid that can be slotted in at various levels. The advantage of the collar is that it ensures adequate draught-proofing and a greater heat can be maintained towards the back of the barbecue. They usually stand on legs and reach to about waist high.

BRAZIER

KETTLE BARBECUES

This type is similar in height to the brazier barbecue and looks like a circular drum with a hinged lid. It is well designed, the draught being effectively controlled by opening and closing one or more holed sliding flanges. A greater, even heat can be maintained for cooking larger items, the kettle acting more like a conventional oven. There is also a large grid area and as the coals are in the centre, there is room round the sides not directly over the heat, where the food can be kept hot. The coals are usually placed on a rack over an ash pan. Together with the space between the rack and the ash pan, the vented air-holes create a good draught, making the barbecue easy to light. Not all kettle barbecues have an internal ash catcher, but this makes for little difference in perform-ance.

KETTLE BARBECUE

CALOR-GAS-OPERATED BARBECUES

These are usually rectangular in shape but you need to have the gas bottle close by and this is heavy to manoeuvre. The coals used are normally lava bricks which have the advantage of taking only ten minutes to ignite, compared with thirty or forty minutes for other types, and there is no subsequent ash. They work well but, to me, this method is not true barbecuing but rather more like cooking on a grill in the kitchen. You can produce an authentic barbecue aroma by dropping a few herbs or, if you can get them, damp wood chippings on to the hot coals.

GAS OPERATED BARBECUE

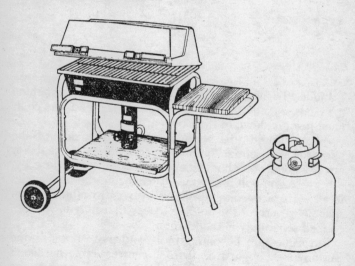

There are of course other types of barbecue including electrically ignited ones and the sophisticated waggon which has many extra refinements including an electrically-driven grill.

WAGGON

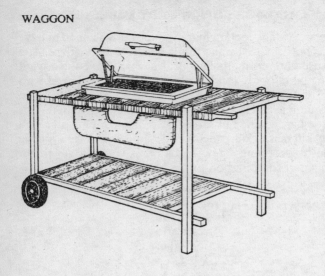

Lidded barbecues can be closed down for dampening the coals and snuffing the fire. If there is no lid, the coals must just die down of their own accord.

I have found that a shelf fixed to the side of the barbecue is essential for putting accessories on; if this is not possible, you should have a wooden table close by, otherwise you will find yourself balancing the accessories in all sorts of unsuitable places. Any extra table or shelf space is so useful for holding dishes that may have been cooked separately in the kitchen.

Barbecues are becoming more and more popular and can now be bought from garden centres, large hardware stores, department stores, specialist barbecue shops and through a growing second-hand market. If, when you buy a second-hand barbecue it is a little messy, take heart, for even a new one gets that way in a relatively short while. When buying a new model watch out for the cheaper types where paint will chip easily; enamelled metal is superior, lasts longer and retains the heat more efficiently. If you do not have a purpose-made cover to go over the barbecue for storage purposes, use a split-open dustbin bag.

LIGHTING THE BARBECUE

Barbecuing is an adult operation and although the children like to help, they should always be given the safer tasks like fetching the coal, and no child should have anything to do with the lit coals or the cooking itself.

There are several different kinds of charcoal suitable for use with a barbecue. Brickettes are available in different guises but I find the oval shape the best. Wood charcoal pieces are made from various woods and have been dried or partly burnt in the preparation process. I found even-shaped pieces of charcoal the best because more air

TYPES OF FUEL

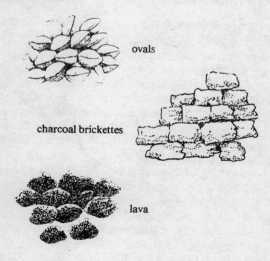

ovals

charcoal brickettes

lava

pockets can be created, thus encouraging the ready flow of flame. Alternatively you can use wood on its own, but this gives off a lot of smoke. It is really a question of trial and error until you find what is best suited to your particular style of cooking.

Arrange only sufficient coal to heat the cooking area you need. If the middle only is to be used just build that small area of fire. First lay the coals flat, extending beyond the cooking area by 1 inch all round. Then heap more coals into a pyramid and light – use solid firelighters, a liquid starter or lighting gel.

Firelighters should not be broken up too small – 2 × 1 inch pieces are the best. A match burns out much too quickly and paper used as a taper burns up and floats away to land on top of the dog, so use a proper taper or a candle which you can hold for longer even though the grease may drop off the end.

LIGHTING THE BARBECUE

insert firelighting brickettes in pieces at least 2″ long × 1″

or squeeze jelly over from tube or sprinkle from bottle

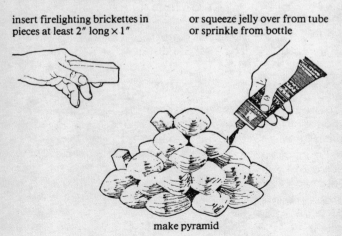

make pyramid

If using lighting gel, squeeze it in fairly large quantities over the coals before igniting and do not be concerned about this possibly tainting the food, for it is manufactured in such a way that it will neither spatter nor smell.

Liquid starters are made especially for barbecues. *Never* pour petrol over the coals, as this would result only in lost eyebrows and third-degree burns. For successful results you must allow a few minutes for the liquid to soak into the coals. If only the surface is dampened, leaping flames will persist for about two minutes, then burn out, leaving the charcoal unlit. It is dangerous to add more liquid starter to seemingly unignited coals because even a faint residual glow could cause the starter to burst into unexpected flames. A drawback to this method of starting is that there is a noticeable smell which seems to permeate any food you might have near the barbecue, and barbecue cognoscenti claim that when a liquid starter has been used, the food tastes of it. However, the addition of herbs will help to disguise this. I use fresh herbs (or pine incense cones which I brought back from America) to create an appetizing smell.

When the fire is alight remove the remainder of the inflammable material to a safe distance.

THE FIRE

The way in which the coals have been arranged, the amount of breeze and also the size and shape of the charcoal influence the time taken to light the fire. The quickest to heat are the gas-ignited lava bricks which do not themselves burn away. Uneven-shaped nuggets take longer to catch but give more even heat, whilst oval or cylindrical pieces are hot in about fifteen minutes and these also give lasting heat. Charcoal tends to burn quickly to a powder so that you need more than you at first think.

When the coals have caught and are flaming nicely you

can then flatten and spread them out (I use a poker for this). Don't start cooking until the embers are really grey all round the bits of coal. The food will only char if put on to cook while the flames are still licking and the coals are red. If you have put enough coal on in the first place the heat will probably last a couple of hours, but you can add ten to twelve brickettes every hour around the edges to keep the fire going provided you can insert them without the food falling in. Forty brickettes would usually be enough for an average barbecue.

To test whether the coals are hot enough put your hand over the coals just above the grid. If you can keep it there for as long as five seconds, the temperature is low; if you can hold it there for three to four seconds, it is medium hot; but if it is only bearable for two seconds, it is hot. On a lidded barbecue, the heat is greater when the lid is lowered. Hot coals are good for searing, for cooking shallow pieces of food; medium heat is best for meat kebabs, vegetables and small items like chicken pieces; and low heat is good for roasts. Cook immediately above the hot white ash (white in the daylight, after dark it will glow red) and from time to time tap the ash off a little.

If you wish to cook over medium heat, but the coals have become too hot, place the food away from the centre of the barbecue and then when cooking is completed, push it right to the edges, where it will stay warm. It is surprising how much you can cook at any one time – much more than you would think possible.

If you need to reactivate the barbecue when it is on its last legs, add a layer of small pieces of coal with more firelighters, but not until there are no distinguishable lumps left.

If you want the fire to become hotter, poke to remove the ash, push the coals together and gently blow by some method (see pages 21–2). Don't poke too much as white ash attracts the heat and should not be destroyed. To make it cooler, prise the coals apart rather than pushing them together and mist with water or, on models which are adjustable, raise the grid. The latter is difficult when there is food on the grid as it tends to fall off, so take the food off first, reposition the grid, then replace the food.

Use a sprinkler or a plant sprayer to put out any flare-ups, and it should be remembered that a handy fire extinguisher never goes amiss in any household situation.

ACCESSORIES

The right barbecue accessories are a must and it's worth looking around to find them. Generally speaking ordinary kitchen tools are not long enough; long-handled tools are needed so that you don't burn your hands every time you approach the coals – tongs, forks, skewers, special fish net or rack, curved basket for grilling whole poultry; and for spit cooking, a special spit which must have two good pronged fixings to insert into the food. This can be operated electrically if power is available in your back-yard.

Brushes are needed for basting and you must have really good oven gloves – individual not double ones. Double-ended oven gloves are dangerous if only one end is used because the dangling part can get caught and cause problems.

A meat thermometer is a useful accessory, particularly for poultry and pork, which must be completely cooked.

Flies are attracted to the smells and light of the barbecue and may zoom in to join you. The best way to rid yourself of these in the dark is to have some kind of strong light away from the cooking area to divert their attention. In the country midges can be a problem, so keep a tube of anti-midge cream close by. It is also a good idea to use barrier cream before starting to cook, as the hands get very ingrained handling the charcoal.

A pair of bellows is handy to perk up a dwindling fire

or, if your lead is long enough, use an electric hair dryer on lowest speed. A drinking straw or the inside cylinder from a roll of paper towels can be used provided you blow from a distance.

Foil, preferably heavy duty or used double, has many barbecue uses, so it is best to buy a big roll. Place a piece of foil in the base of the Hibachi or picnic barbecue so that the ash can be easily gathered up and thrown away. If used in the kettle grill, be careful not to cover the vents. Foil is of no use in the gas grill except for a covering directly on top of the lava bricks to help burn off the grease afterwards. If you wish to turn a brazier into a kettle grill, make a dome out of foil – this would need to be several thicknesses thick to hold its shape. Reshape wire coat hangers to make a frame.

Foil is of great value in barbecue cookery for lining, tenting or wrapping. Cover the tables with foil to protect

HOW TO MAKE A DOMED LID

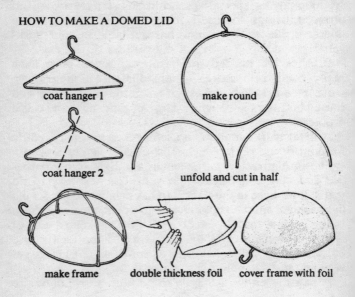

coat hanger 1

make round

coat hanger 2

unfold and cut in half

make frame

double thickness foil

cover frame with foil

the surfaces from grease, then at the end of the operation you can gather everything up and put it in the dustbin.

Vermiculite chippings as used by builders if put in a single layer underneath the coals will absorb quite a lot of fat and also help to reduce flare-ups.

CLEANING

Empty out the ash only when cold and wipe around the barbecue with newspaper to get out the worst of the grease. Special barbecue cleaner is quite effective and a brush and scraper, specially designed for barbecues, make life a lot easier. Use rubber gloves to prevent dirt and grease sticking to the hands. Don't make too much of a chore out of cleaning the barbecue if it is going to be used fairly frequently; on the other hand do not let it get so dirty that grease builds up, as this makes smoke – although it has been said that a little burnt-on grease adds flavour next time around.

Clean the outside of the barbecue, when cold, with a cloth and washing-up liquid, then polish dry.

2

Cooking Methods

Some foods can be cooked without any prior treatment. Some will need a little preparation which can be done while you are waiting for the coals to heat.

MARINADING AND TENDERIZING

Meat and poultry in particular benefit from a soak in a marinade which not only tenderizes but also adds an individual flavour. The marinade tenderizes because of the reaction of the acids with the meat enzymes. A marinade is unnecessary for tenderizing better cuts such as rump or fillet steak but it does add flavour. If you want to tenderize cheaper-quality steaks, marinading is not the answer because it encourages the meat juices to seep and this would make the meat dry when cooked. It is much better to use a commercial tenderizing powder derived from papaya. However, do not be too generous with the papaya powder and do not apply it more than thirty minutes in advance or the meat will change its texture.

A less effective method, one which does not soften the surface of the meat, is to prick thoroughly with a fork, so that the heat can penetrate the surface more rapidly. Mince has been tenderized by the very act of cutting the meat into small morsels, but a hefty whack with the flat side of a cleaver is often sufficient to break down a few tough fibres.

In addition to tenderizing and giving flavour, a marinade can be used for basting, to keep food moist, and sometimes may be served as a sauce. Not only meat and poultry, but fish, vegetables and fruit are frequently pre-soaked in a marinade to enhance flavour and juiciness. See Chapter 10 for marinade suggestions.

Use fresh herbs as an alternative to marinading by slashing the meat and poking in the herbs with a skewer. You can throw a few garlic cloves or onion pieces or fresh herbs on to the coals to give an attractive aroma towards the end of the cooking time.

THE FIVE WAYS TO BARBECUE

Grilling

Grilling is one of the most popular barbecue methods and indeed the easiest. The commonest form of grilling is by cooking directly on the grid. Unfortunately fatty meats will drip on to the hot coals and cause spitting and flare-ups. To reduce this risk, fatty foods are generally grilled by 'indirect' cooking. To do this a foil dish or baking tin is embedded in the centre of the coals and the food is put on

INDIRECT COOKING

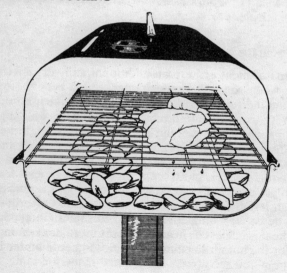

the grid over that. The fat will then drip into the pan below, while the food (e.g. duck) is heated from the coals around the side. To calm a flare-up generously sprinkle salt on the flames and into the fat.

Any foods that can be grilled, shallow fried, dry roasted (without being in a pan of fat), foil-baked (including steaks; chops; burgers; sausages; whole poultry; whole carcases of meat; fish, either whole or fillets; vegetables and fruit) can be cooked on the barbecue.

Brush the food or the grid with oil before grilling and adjust the heat by cooking closer or further away from the hottest part of the coals. Thick fatty cuts should be cooked over indirect heat (i.e. place a foil pan underneath the food in the centre of the coals). Meat, with the exception of pork, should not be salted before cooking as salt draws out the juices. It is preferable to brush with sauce after the meat is sealed and towards the end of the cooking time. Put seasoning in the cavity of poultry before cooking; score the skin of a pork joint and insert salt in the cuts to produce crispier crackling.

Roasting on the grid

All joints of meat acquire an additional and very special flavour when roasted on the barbecue and benefit similarly from indirect cooking. Use a drip pan which is deep enough to contain all the fat because it is well nigh impossible to empty the pan during the cooking period. The difference between roasting and grilling is simply that grilling is carried out on two sides only, while a roast, because it is thicker, has to be turned several times for all sides to get even cooking. Roasting on the grid is quicker although less flavoursome than spit roasting. Grid roasts should be cooked on a covered grid so that a greater all-round heat is achieved, but it is important to have enough room for the hot air to circulate. A closed kettle barbecue is ideal but you can always use a home-made foil tent.

The coals should be at medium heat. Joints cooked over hot coals will burn on the outside, while the inside remains raw. A meat thermometer used properly will guarantee perfect results, but to save looking at this too often and letting in the cold air, insert it into the centre of the meat three-quarters of the way through the cooking time. The thermometer must always be inserted in the thickest part of the meat and not against bone or in the fat, or the temperature will mis-read. The internal temperature of a joint of beef should reach 60°C (140°F) for rare and 70°C (160°F) for well done. Underdone beef takes about 20 minutes per pound and well-done beef about 25 minutes per pound. Pork must always be thoroughly cooked – the temperature must reach 75°C (170°F). For chicken, 85° to 90°C (185° to 190°F) is the recommended temperature. An additional test for checking that the chicken is cooked is by twisting the leg to see if the bone comes away easily and the juices are running clear. You can prevent chicken wing tips and legs from over-roasting by wrapping them with foil.

Have enough spare coals on the side to poke through the bars close to the fire to prevent the heat from dying down over the lengthy cooking period. Leave meat joints to stand for five minutes before carving or, if rare, all the juices will tumble out, leaving the meat dry.

The best way to cook a crown roast is to put it directly into the drip pan on top of the grill. The stuffing must be cooked separately. Do not use the indirect method.

A roasting rack is very useful when the joints are round and thus likely to roll about. The meat can be turned much more easily in the curved cradle, which is placed on the grid. You will not, however, be able to use the meat thermometer, as each time the joint and the thermometer are repositioned, juices will seep out through the resulting hole.

ROASTING RACK

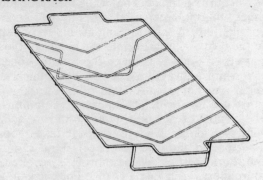

Spit Roasting

Only barbecues with a special fitment are suitable for spit roasting, although you can use the spit in the grid for roasts in order to turn them more easily.

A rotisserie can be either manually or electrically operated. I must admit I have not tried the latter in my back-yard and I haven't found a gas barbecue incorporating a rotisserie.

Spit roasting is useful when two or three joints or chickens are being cooked simultaneously. Large carcases such as sucking pig or a side of lamb are superb for a special occasion. Really the best way to cook these is over a large home-built barbecue. On these the spitting, splashing and flare-ups won't matter because the cook is unlikely to be standing over the cooking and the guests will be well back from the sparks.

Turkey is not recommended for spit roasting as it is just too big and the inside would not be cooked by the time the outside was done. It is not even any good trying to cook one on a massive home-built barbecue because of the texture of the meat.

SPIT ROASTING

The advantage of spit roasting is that it makes more of a spectacle out of barbecuing, and even if the grid roast may be more efficiently cooked, it won't achieve the crisp exterior of the spit roast. The disadvantage is that you really cannot do anything else at the same time.

A spit is a long metal rod which is inserted through the centre of the joint, and is fixed into position by two clamps. One clamp must be positioned at the handle end before inserting into the joint. An important point at this stage is to make sure the spit balances before placing it in the barbecue. Push the prongs very close to the joint or the joint will afterwards either fall off or not turn round with the spit as the rod turns. You can tighten the screws of the prongs with pliers to make sure they are really firm, but never try to tighten them after the metal has heated.

There is another type of spit available; this is fixed to a basket which encloses the joint.

To fix poultry on the spit, thrust the rod through the loose skin of the neck end as close to the backbone as possible. If you are cooking several chickens at the same time, place them all head to tail so that they all face the same direction and use birds of the same shape.

You must never cook chicken with the giblets in, so always thaw out frozen birds and remove the plastic-wrapped giblets before you start. You can season poultry before cooking, but do not stuff. Make certain there are enough coals for the whole operation. First turn the spit a couple of times manually, to see if there is any flapping of loose skin, then tie the legs and wings very securely.

Poultry will drip a lot, so you must have a drip pan large enough to receive the fat from all the birds, if cooking several. The coals should be medium hot. At the end of cooking time, the birds will require a 15-minute resting period before carving.

With fattier cuts of meat, the joint may become unbalanced once the fat has dripped off, and this should be taken into account when you start. Put the spit in the centre of the lean part rather than in the centre of the whole joint. Have a slightly higher pile of brickettes at the back of the barbecue in order to maximize the heat and place the drip pan slightly in front of the spit. Trim off the excess fat first so that only about half an inch is left on a joint.

Foil cookery and cooking in the coals

Foil cooking has many advantages, the major one being that all the juices are trapped inside. It also keeps out flies and dust. Heavy-duty or double-thickness foil will prevent the outside of the food burning before the inside is cooked. To help prevent sticking, lightly brush with oil before wrapping the food.

Some foods can eat their way through the foil. Among these are items of high onion content, and rice which pits through the foil if left for any length of time. It will not make any difference which side of the foil you place against the food, but if making a tent it is better to place the reflecting side inwards.

There are three methods of wrapping food in foil. The first I call 'flat fold'. Place the food in the middle of a large square of foil and draw the top and bottom edges well up above the centre of the food, then fold over once or twice to obtain a good seal. Next take the two folded ends and turn them over a few times. If you will be lifting the foil off the coals with tongs, make one longer (empty) end. For cooking delicate food such as fish, use foil to make a couple of bracelets so that you can lift out both ends at the same time.

FOIL WRAPPING flat fold

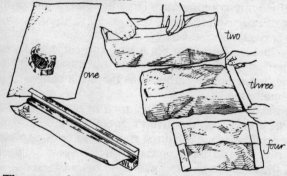

The second method is the 'dolly-bag' method. This is not so airtight but is better for round items such as apples and onions. Just put the food in the centre of the foil, draw up the four corners and twist the top so that the sides close up. This does not make a juice-containing seal.

Thirdly, if there are no particular problems about the food to be placed in the foil, just wrap loosely as if storing apples in newspaper.

Foil can be used to line the grid when cooking by a grill-fry method, and is useful for shaping into drip trays

FOIL WRAPPING dolly bag

provided there are enough thicknesses. Use foil for tenting during cooking or after cooking for holding in the heat. If you are cooking for a large number of guests, foil tenting can be used to keep food warm, so that everyone can be served at the same time.

Two cautions here: Do not attempt to cut on foil, as it slits through so easily, and do not use plastic-lined foil pudding basins on the barbecue as there is a danger of the plastic melting.

Foil-wrapped cooking can be done in two ways on the barbecue – either on the grid or directly in the coals. On those occasions when a baking tray would not be suitable (light trays tend to buckle and non-stick trays will deteriorate in the extreme heat), make a foil one instead.

Cooking in the coals is most suitable for vegetables with skins, such as potatoes, aubergines, corn on the cob, onions, green peppers, etc. Before wrapping, rub slightly with oil. Do not try to cook in the middle of the fire (which will be too hot) but use the outer area, pushing the coals away if you think cooking is taking place too quickly. This method is not suitable for meat, unless vegetables are included to provide moisture.

If cooking a whole chicken in the coals, cover all over with a 1 cm (½ in) layer of sea or rock salt and wrap very

COOKING IN THE COALS

tightly in double- or treble-thickness foil – this keeps in the flavour remarkably well. The recipe should not be wasted on a frozen chicken – buy a special fresh bird from the butcher. Cooking time is about 20 minutes per pound.

Frying

Frying is possible only if a thin layer of fat is used. Deep frying would cause too much spattering and be quite dangerous as the fat would fall on the coals. Merely grease a heavy iron pan or griddle lightly – cooking then becomes a cross between baking above the barbecue and shallow frying. If you are cooking fatty meat (for example, sausages) a frying pan can be very useful to prevent the fat dripping into the coals. Coals must be hot for barbecue frying.

You should fry as you carry out any other cooking on the barbecue: by moving the pan from the middle to the side, in order to control the heat. The disadvantage is that you will not get the typical barbecue flavour. However, if you wish to use a little sauce to go with the meat, it is easy to make one using the residual frying juices in the pan (see the recipe for Hopi Chile Rolls page 12. This is a type of fry-bake).

Items that are very dry, like vegetable nutburgers, are better for being fried. Fried bread, too, cooks well.

All sorts of subsidiary items, like baked beans, can be put on the grid beside the frying pan, either in a foil dish or in the unlidded can.

What could start off a summer morning better than to have breakfast in the traditional way, but out of doors? Make coffee and put it in a Thermos flask to avoid running in and out of the kitchen.

On skewers

Skewered food is usually, but not invariably, marinated. Kebabs must be well brushed either with oil or the juice they have been marinated in, or with a sauce. Try to use a large dish for marinating so that the marinade will cover the meat when threaded on to the skewers. Alternatively, transfer the marinade to a tall narrow jug and let the skewers stand upright in the juice.

Buy skewers with handles that are wooden and that won't get hot, and don't thread small skewers for a single serving. Long skewers which can go from one side of the grid to the other and which hold two or three servings are best. When cooking sausages, either insert the skewer through the length of the sausage, fitting on as many as will go, or use two skewers threading the sausages rather like steps on a ladder. You will find them easier to turn over.

Skewers should be turned frequently while cooking, and when done can be placed on the side of the grill to keep warm. To serve from the skewers, remove the food with a fork, placing the tip of the skewer on the plate and lowering the skewer to a more horizontal position as the items are removed.

Do not put pieces of meat too close to each other on the skewers as you will not get an even heat when meat cubes are packed one against the other. Separate them with interspersing vegetables. The best size of meat to use is 2.5–3.75 cm (1–1½ in) cubes. Meat balls should be refrigerated before threading on to skewers.

COOKING ON SKEWERS

When skewering mushrooms, cut off the stalk flush with the cap and then press the skewer through the point where the stalk has joined the cap. If you are not using baby tomatoes, cut them crosswise and not through the stalk. Arrange those items which cook the quickest nearest the handle – they will then be furthest away from the heat.

Skewers can be heated directly over the coals as there is little problem with spattering.

Fruit is quite delicious when cooked on skewers. Baste with sauce containing a high quantity of butter to prevent the flesh drying out.

3

Cooking the Basic Foods

The foods most usually cooked on the barbecue are sausages, steaks, burgers, chops, chicken pieces, and less usually, fish and vegetables. Here are a few tips to help you get the best results with these basic items.

SAUSAGES

Sausages should be pricked to prevent bursting and so that the fat can drain off during barbecuing. It is not advisable to cook sausages over fierce heat as the outsides would burn while the insides would be raw and the colour very uneven.

Cook sausages individually or threaded on skewers (either lengthwise or in ladder fashion between two skewers) which makes turning easier.

Very fatty sausages are best cooked by the indirect method to prevent flare-ups over a drip tray set in medium coals; however, if you prefer, much of the fat can be removed before barbecuing either by (a) putting the sausages into cold water in a saucepan on the hob, bringing to the boil and then draining; or (b) microwaving on high for a few seconds. These methods both help to remove excess fat and par-cook to reduce the overall cooking time. Frozen sausages should be microwaved for one minute per sausage.

Sausages can be fried on the barbecue, in which case the heat should be higher.

Once sausages are cooked they can be kept hot on the sides of the grill, but if they do go cold, they can be served with one of the dips in the recipe section or reheated in the microwave oven.

Average cooking time for sausages is about 15 minutes, pork sausages taking longer than beef. Turn them continually for even browning and cooking. Frankfurters and the like take only 5–10 minutes, cooked directly over medium coals. Serve with dips or slit them open and insert one of the flavoured butters (see page 151).

The required cooking time is increased when sausage meat is made into burgers. Cook these over medium rather than hot coals.

I don't advise very thin chipolata-type sausages being cooked directly on a grid as they tend to burn on the outside almost immediately. Tiny cocktail and thin sausages are better when cooked either in a foil dish over medium coals or in the frying pan.

You can always make your own sausages if you get chitterlings (the small intestines of the pig extruded thinly into film). Some electric mixers have sausage-filling attachments. You can then make sausages with your own mixes; the cooking time will depend on the content.

STEAKS

Thick steaks, 2.5–5 cm (1–2 in) thick are best for barbecue cooking. Prime rump or fillet need no previous preparation, but less expensive cuts like sirloin, porterhouse or entrecôte, although they still cook quite well, are better if they have been marinated. To help the tenderizing process, slash them deeply, diagonally across the grain, on both sides.

I don't think fillet steak is a good barbecue choice except for special dinner parties for a few people. By the time you get round to cooking a large number, these expensive steaks would be spoilt and indistinguishable from cheaper cuts of meat. Minute steaks cook well because they are so thin and require only a couple of minutes, as their name suggests. Brush thin steaks during

cooking with flavoured butters which have been prepared
with herbs some time previously so that the herbs infuse
the butter. It is not advisable to brush steaks with melted
butter and then sprinkle the herbs on, for the herbs will
then just char and not flavour the steaks. With thick
meat you can push the herbs right inside the slashes
before cooking, although any herbs left on the edge will
still char.

Before cooking steaks, trim away excess fat to avoid
flare-ups. The remaining fat should be slashed through
until the knife reaches the lean meat, to prevent curling.
Brush the steaks with oil, or brush the grid, to prevent
sticking. A thick oil such as olive oil is better than a thin
sunflower oil.

Place the steaks directly over hot coals, turning over
after a short while so that both sides are sealed. They must
be turned again half-way through cooking.

Always use tongs for turning – forks with their sharp
prongs allow the juices to run out which is bad for steaks
and reduces their flavour. If some eaters want rare and
some medium, and you have not been able to judge the
correct cooking time, persuade them to swap their steaks
rather then continually prodding the meat. The best way
to test for degree of cooking is to press with a clean
finger or the handle of a knife. Resilience and firmness
indicate the amount of doneness – the more cooked, the
firmer the meat. But remember that firmness also equals
toughness.

Over hot coals the cooking times for a 2.5 cm (1 in)
thick steak are:

rare	10 minutes
medium	15 minutes
well done	20 minutes

BURGERS

Burgers are best when not too thick; 1–1.8 cm (½–¾ in) burgers will cook more quickly and evenly. As it is difficult to achieve even doneness with thick burgers, cook two average ones and sandwich them together with cheese, tomato or salami.

Brush the burgers well with oil or butter and cook very thin burgers over hot coals, thicker ones over medium coals. Burgers can also be fried over hot coals but the barbecue flavour will be lacking and you will have to sprinkle them with barbecue seasoning to get the right effect.

Giant burgers or meat loaves must be cooked covered, either with the barbecue lid or a foil tent. Cook in the same way as steaks, first sealing each side for one minute or so. Do not turn them over more than once during cooking – flip them over with a fish slice, rather than using tongs, to prevent them falling to pieces.

You can shape hamburgers with a ready-made press or make your own burger ring out of a 30 cm (12 in) length of foil. Fold over and over lengthwise so that there are several thicknesses, shape into a ring then press the meat mixture into it. Do not press too firmly, as mince must breathe and if too dense does not cook well. If you are making your own burger mixture in your processor, do not overmix as the same problem will arise. It is important to retain aeration. Another point, if you make your own burgers: after mixing and shaping they should be refrigerated to firm up.

In Chapter 10 there are quite a few barbecue sauce recipes, but I strongly recommend the use of butters on burgers as well, as it is a pity to restrict yourself to sauces. Don't be put off by the hotness of our magnificent Mexiburger recipe – you can always leave out the chillis. Brush butters on the burgers in the same way as for steaks.

Burgers are usually served in soft rolls, but as a change try putting them in pitta bread accompanied with sauces and side salads. If you do this, cut the burgers in half before cooking to make them easier to insert. It will make little difference to the cooking times.

Most people like their burgers well done and this takes up to 15 minutes. Medium-cooked burgers will take 8–10 minutes. Thin commercial burgers will cook even more quickly.

CHOPS

Chops can be cooked directly on the grid; in foil; fried; or by any of those methods after marinating. When buying chops for barbecuing bear in mind the cooking method you are going to use. Lean chops with a covering of fat are the best choice for cooking on the grid; choose chops with fat amongst the lean (known as marbling).

Lamb chops can be loin, chump or best-end neck. Loin chops are thick; chump are even thicker, without a tail; and best-end neck are most useful as they have nice long tails for picking up.

Lamb chops will take 15–20 minutes to cook. It is the thickness that decides rather than the quantity of meat on the chop. Pork chops take about twice as long. Cook over medium coals. If there is no bone, roll up the chop and thread horizontally to make a noisette chop. Coat chops in different butters to give a choice of flavour.

Spare rib pork chops (these are not Chinese spare ribs) should be cooked, covered, over low coals for 1–1¼ hours. Thread them on skewers as if using a tacking stitch (winding the skewers in and out). They are particularly good cooked on a spit when they can be secured by the prongs at either end.

Never serve pork rare – the juices must run clear when the meat is tested. To do this, insert the tip of a sharp knife into the centre of the flesh. This prodding will in no way affect any further cooking – only beef reacts badly to this treatment.

CHICKEN PIECES

Chicken pieces that are marinated in oil alone tend to soften and go pappy. There is no need to use oil in a marinade for chicken.

When the pieces are to be grilled, first well oil the grid and the chicken portions and baste frequently during cooking, which should be done on the sides of the grid. Drumsticks or thighs will take 20–25 minutes over medium coals. As with pork, test with a sharp knife or skewer to make certain the juices run clear. No meats – particularly chicken – should be cooked straight from the freezer.

To give added flavour, the chicken pieces can be impregnated with herbs by slashing through the skin and inserting your chosen herb(s). This is particularly good for chicken quarters, e.g. breast on the bone. The flavour is retained more efficiently if the pieces are cooked in a closed barbecue or tented in foil.

Duck pieces should be cooked by the indirect method over medium coals. As duck is full of fat this method enables it to drip out to a considerable extent. Turn the pieces over every 10 minutes.

Poussin, which is dry-textured, should also be cooked by the indirect method. Because of its dryness put butter or a small piece of Stilton cheese into the cavity before starting to cook.

Chicken or duck can be grilled in the basket. A closed basket can be improvised so that both basket and its contents can be turned easily during cooking. Brush with your chosen sauce towards the end of cooking time.

Always cook whole chicken in a closed cooker, covered with a foil tent, or in a basket. If you only have a brazier-type barbecue, make a half-hood of foil which can be propped up against the collar of the barbecue.

All these poultry roasts can be cooked in foil packets although this method takes a little longer.

As chicken pieces are slow to cook, if you are cooking quite a few you will find it a boon to first par-cook them in the microwave oven; otherwise pre-cook in the conventional oven.

FISH

Fish steaks should be cut thickly. A halibut steak 1.8 cm (¾ in) thick cooked over medium coals will take about 15 minutes. Cook the steaks directly on a very-well-buttered grid covered with double thickness foil, or in foil packets, or in the frying pan. If cooking fish fillets directly on the grid, use special fish baskets or foil bracelets as the flesh so easily becomes damaged. For whole fish make two foil bracelets and place one near the head and one near the waist; curl little loops at each end for easy lifting and you will then be able to turn the fish over without any trouble. Fish is cooked when the flesh flakes easily and is opaque.

Shellfish can be bought cooked or uncooked. The pre-cooked kind need only a light brushing with melted butter before heating. Uncooked shellfish need lots and lots of basting during cooking. If shellfish pieces are large enough they can be threaded on to skewers.

FRUIT AND VEGETABLES

Fruit and vegetables can be cooked on the barbecue either skewered, in foil or fried. Some vegetables require blanching or par-cooking beforehand to shorten the barbecuing time. Timings are very important if items are not to fall apart during the cooking process, or alternatively dry up. You will find more information about fruit and vegetables in the various chapters – suffice it to say here that very soft varieties should be treated with care, so that they do not fall off the skewers or become mushy, tomatoes and bananas being the chief sufferers.

You will obviously know how much your own family are likely to eat but for barbecue parties, you can anticipate that the average person will tend to eat at least two and probably three cooked items. They will also eat all the side salads that are offered.

Although it is easy to say you will have a spur-of-the-moment barbecue – you've probably seen on television how at the drop of a hat the barbecue is lit and the cooking begins in moments – don't forget it really takes 30–40 minutes to prepare and light a barbecue. The 'spur-of-the-moment' barbecue must therefore be prepared some hours before.

4

Menu Section

To get the most out of a barbecue, begin your preparations well in advance. Although the coals may take up to 45 minutes to heat adequately, unless you have someone to help you this is insufficient time for any lengthy preparation out of doors as you will constantly be popping in and out to make sure the fire is making the desired progress. Then, when the coals reach the right temperature, it's highly likely that you won't have the food ready to cook. Last-minute touches and dishes that have to be ready at a specified time can often be slotted in between lighting and the moment when the coals are ready. Meat which requires tenderizing and fish, poultry and vegetables can be soaked in a marinade many hours in advance. Savoury butters, basting sauces, dips and dressings can all be pre-prepared to some extent. Prepare salads, peel vegetables and half or fully cook soups and brush dry foods with oil.

Sometimes it will be helpful to par-cook plain foods, such as sausages and chicken pieces, so that you can eat soon after the coals are hot. On the other hand, if a large menu is being served, leave these foods completely raw – then you can enjoy watching them cook while you eat the preceding dish.

When planning your menu, first look closely at the recipes. Work out how much can be done well in advance and what can be prepared immediately before lighting the barbecue or during the time it will take for the coals to catch and turn into the vital grey ash. It's worth spending time on this, because it's only then that you can judge if you can cope with your choice. If not, change to a menu that *will* work. Consider too, is the barbecue going to be large enough for the numbers taking part and will they be eating all at the same time? Have you chosen one single cooking method, i.e. only grills or fries?

With a little forethought you can get away with using quite a small barbecue. Two methods of cooking may be better than one, e.g. foil packets can be put into the coals just before cooking grills on the grid. You can then use the entire grid surface for the grills or skewers, pushing the cooked portions to the sides as they become ready. It doesn't matter if these are piled up. The foil packets underneath do not greatly affect the heat of the coals.

If you wish, some dishes can be prepared in the kitchen to be brought hot and ready straight to the barbecue. These will need only one small corner of the grid to keep them warm. Another method is to introduce a half-cooked fry which can then be finished on the barbecue within moments of serving up the grilled items.

So that the whole meal can be streamlined, remove the foil packets from the coals *after* the grid has been cleared. There will now be space and time for other quick-cooking items to be barbecued.

If you decide to spit roast, most of the other dishes (with the exception of barbecued desserts) will have to be cooked in the kitchen.

The menus that follow should give you a guide to planning, but of course you do not have to keep rigorously to them. The more elaborate the meal, the more essential it is to prepare several hours beforehand. It is all right to plonk chops and chicken pieces straight on to the grill, but specialist items require to be well organized in the kitchen substantially in advance.

In their first efforts with a barbecue, most people cook the basics such as chops, burgers, sausages and chicken pieces and are inclined to brush everything with the same barbecue sauce, either from a bottle or a quick combination of tomato purée, brown sugar, vinegar and Worcestershire sauce. There is certainly nothing wrong with doing this, but there's more to barbecuing than a single flavour. It's easy to vary the sauces or indeed the marinades with very little ingenuity. As soon as you get the hang of barbecuing, try out your favourite basics, but use a different barbecue sauce or marinade with each batch – you'll notice the variation in the flavour.

In the recipe sections there are plenty of suggestions for marinades, dips and sauces, things to start with and accompanying dishes that can be cooked in the kitchen. All these different ideas will help to produce a rounded menu. The aim of the menu section is to suggest various combinations that are both usual and unusual, but always exciting and appetizing, while being within the bounds of possibility. They don't involve any more prowess than the basics you started with.

PRACTICE DINNER

MENU 1

	Method	Heat & Time on Barbecue	Work Plan
Lamb Chops	Grid	Medium 15–20 mins	Wipe, trim and brush with oil a few hours ahead; remove from the refrigerator 30 minutes ahead.
Jacket Potatoes (p 104)	Conventional oven		Bake in the conventional oven 45 minutes ahead; wrap in foil and put on sides of grid as soon as coals are alight.
Garlic Beans and Mushrooms (p 179)	Conventional hob		Cook a few hours ahead of time; leave in covered saucepan; reheat while lamb chops are cooking, then transfer to barbecue in saucepan.
Green Salad with Vinaigrette Dressing	Kitchen preparation		Wash, dry and arrange in bowl 1 hour before meal; prepare dressing up to 1 month ahead and store in bottle or covered jar; shake thoroughly, add to salad and toss while lamb is cooking.
Fresh Berry Crumble (p 200)	Conventional oven		Make crumble up to 2 days ahead of time and store in covered containers; whip cream, mix with fruits and layer with crumble up to 2 hours before serving; keep in refrigerator until required.

Cooking Count-Down 1. Put baked potatoes in oven. 2. Wash salad and put in bowl. 3. Light coals. 4. Wrap potatoes in foil and put on grid. 5. Cook chops. 6. Reheat beans. 7. Toss salad.

MENU 2

GERMAN DINNER

	Method	Heat & Time on Barbecue	Work Plan
Pork Chops in Cider and Clove Butter (p 77)	Grid	Medium 30 minutes	Marinade several hours before; prepare the clove butter 1 hour before; reduce the marinade and spread over chops; spread with butter.
Bavarian Red Cabbage (p 182)	Conventional hob		Cook several hours ahead and reheat just before serving.
Boiled New Potatoes	Conventional hob		Scrub ahead of time.
Honey Bananas (p 98)	Foil on grid	Medium 15 minutes	Prepare 1 hour ahead of time.

Cooking Count-Down 1. Light coals. 2. Bring chops and butter outside. 3. Heat cabbage over gentle heat in kitchen. 4. Bring water to boil for potatoes. 5. Put potatoes to cook over gentle heat. 6. Cook chops. 7. Bring cabbage and potatoes to barbecue in suitable dishes. 8. Put bananas to cook when serving chops.

MENU 3   BRITISH DINNER No. 1

	Method	Heat & Time on Barbecue	Work Plan
Cream of Tomato Soup (p 191)	Conventional hob		Make the soup ahead of time and refrigerate.
Mini Roasts (p 85)	Grid	Hot 20 minutes	Recut and tie 1 × 1.25 kg (3 lb) joint if butcher will not do it; brush with oil just before cooking.
Chip Kebabs (p 126)	Skewers on grid	Hot 10 minutes	Thread on skewers and refrigerate.
Coleslaw (p 171)	Kitchen preparation		Make up few hours ahead and put in serving dishes.
Deep-dish Apple Pie (p 209)	Conventional oven		Make and bake ahead of time or prepare and set to bake after lighting the coals.

Cooking Count-Down 1. Light coals. 2. Set pie to bake. 3. Reheat soup. 4. Set joints to cook. 5. After 15 minutes cook chip kebabs. 6. Serve apple pie at end of meal.

MENU 4   COUNTRY DINNER

	Method	Heat & Time on Barbecue	Work Plan
Lemon-Marinaded Sausages (p 114)	Fry	Hot 15 minutes	Prick sausages and marinate up to 8 hours ahead.
Courgettes with Fresh Herbs (p 180)	Conventional hob		Prepare courgettes and marinate up to 6 hours ahead.
Foil-baked Corn on the Cob (p 102)	Foil in coals	Medium 15–20 minutes	Prepare and wrap 6–8 hours ahead.
Raspberries with Strawberry Sauce (p 205)	Kitchen preparation		Prepare fruit and liquidize strawberries several hours ahead and pour over raspberries in individual glasses.

Cooking Count-Down 1. Light coals. 2. Complete desserts. 3. Collect frying pan and butter. 4. Put corn in coals to cook. 5. Bring courgettes in pan to barbecue and finish cooking. 6. Cook sausages in pan on barbecue. 7. Serve sausages and courgettes. 8. Retrieve and serve corn. 9. Serve raspberries.

MENU 5

BURGER AND SALADS

	Method	Heat & Time on Barbecue	Work Plan
Hovis Turkey Loaves (p 78)	Grid	Medium 45–60 minutes	A few hours ahead mix ingredients together and refrigerate; make tomato paste and coat the burgers once and then refrigerate; 30 minutes ahead of time remove from refrigerator and coat with remaining tomato paste.
Bacon Rashers	Grid	Medium 5 minutes	Remove from refrigerator 30 minutes ahead.
Beef, Cheese and Pickle Burgers (p 81)	Grid	Medium 15–20 minutes	A few hours ahead make up mixture and shape into burgers, coat and refrigerate; remove from refrigerator 30 minutes ahead.
Soft Buns			
Homely Baked Beans (p 181)	Conventional hob		Make in advance and reheat on barbecue.
Aubergine Salad (p 168)	Kitchen preparation		Make 12 hours in advance.
Mushroom Salad (p 167)	Kitchen preparation		Make up just before serving.
Tomato Salad (p 167)	Kitchen preparation		Make up 2–3 hours before serving and refrigerate.
Treacle Tart (p 202)	Conventional oven		Make in advance if to be served cold; if not, reheat just before serving.

(Menu 5 continued overleaf)

(Menu 5 continued)

Cooking Count-Down 1. Light coals 1¾ hours ahead of your eating time. 2. Start the Hovis Turkey Loaves. 3. Complete salads. 4. Cut the buns. 5. Put beans and sauce in foil dishes. 6. Check that you have brush at the ready. 7. Have a drink. 8. Start the Beef, Cheese and Pickle Burgers. 9. Cook the bacon rashers 5 minutes before turkey loaves are ready. 10. Serve turkey loaves. 11. Put burgers in buns and warm on barbecue grid while cooking the bacon. 12. Put treacle tart to reheat.

MENU 6   BRITISH DINNER No. 2

	Method	Heat & Time on Barbecue	Work Plan
Beetroot Soup (p 193)	Conventional hob		Make soup without soured cream up to 24 hours ahead; reheat and add cream before serving or if serving cold, stir in soured cream without reheating at any time.
Triple Lamb Chops en Papillote (p 101)	Foil on grid	Medium 30 minutes	Prepare and wrap one or two hours ahead of time.
Steak with Horseradish Butter (p 153)	Grid	Hot – see steak chart	Trim steaks as long as you like ahead of time, refrigerate; remove from refrigerator 30 minutes before cooking; make sauce up to 2 days ahead and refrigerate; spread sauce on steak just before or after cooking.
Jacket Potatoes (p 104)	Conventional oven or Foil in coals	Medium	Bake 45 minutes ahead and finish on barbecue or put into coals as soon as they are hot and grey.
Skewered Vegetables (p 129)	Skewer on grid	Medium 5–35 minutes according to vegetable	Prepare a few hours in advance and put on skewers.
Chocolate-stuffed Bananas with Crème de Cacao (p 97)	Foil in coals	10 minutes	Prepare and wrap in foil 2 hours ahead of time; cook foil packets after main grid used or while eating main course.

Cooking Count-Down 1. Prepare or par-cook potatoes and wrap. 2. Light coals. 3. Reheat soup or serve cold. 4. Put potatoes in coals. 5. Set chops to cook. 6. Cook steaks. 7. Cook vegetables. 8. Serve potatoes after meat is dished up. 9. Put bananas in coals.

MENU 7   DELICATE DINNER

	Method	Heat & Time on Barbecue	Work Plan
Iced Cucumber Soup (p 193)	Conventional hob		Make and refrigerate a few hours in advance.
Trout with Sorrel Sauce (p 80)	Grid	Medium 20 minutes	Make sauce in advance, cover and refrigerate; prepare fish for cooking 1 hour ahead and wrap.
Emerald Salad (p 165)	Kitchen preparation		Make ahead of time and refrigerate; garnish just before serving.
Duchesse Potatoes (p 177)	Conventional oven		Cook and mash potatoes, pipe and brush potatoes with butter and egg a few hours ahead.
Crêpes Suzette (p 116)	Fry	Medium – a few minutes	A few hours ahead of time make pancakes; prepare orange sauce, cover and set aside; measure out butter; prepare sugar shaker and have brandy bottle handy.

Cooking Count-Down 1. Light coals. 2. Garnish salad. 3. Reheat sorrel sauce and transfer to foil dish. 4. Put potatoes in conventional oven to heat and brown. 5. Cook fish and put sauce on side of barbecue to keep warm. 6. Bring potatoes to barbecue. 7. Serve fish, salad and potatoes. 8. Clear dishes. 9. Cook crêpes suzette.

MENU 8

DUCK DINNER

	Method	Heat & Time on Barbecue	Work Plan
Gazpacho (p 194)	Kitchen preparation		Prepare soup up to 24 hours ahead; prepare croûtons up to 24 hours ahead and store in an air-tight container; a few hours ahead get out tureen, soup ladle, bowl for croûtons and soup bowls.
Spit-roast Duck with Deep South Sauce (p 89)	Spit	Medium 2–3 hours	Wash and truss the duck and keep in the refrigerator; have the spit and clips ready nearby.
Saffron Rice (p 184)	Conventional hob		Cook up to 24 hours in advance if storing in refrigerator; freezer-stored rice can be prepared up to a month ahead.
Fresh Spinach Salad with Sesame Dressing (p 172)	Kitchen preparation		Wash, shred and dry spinach up to 2 hours ahead of time; mix dressing ingredients together; have salad bowl to hand.
Sliced Fresh Mango with Limes (p 208)	Kitchen preparation		Prepare several hours ahead; cover and refrigerate.

Cooking Count-Down 1. Light coals. 2. Fix roast on spit and set to cook. 3. During last half hour pour soup into tureen and put croûtons in bowl. 4. Reheat rice. 5. During last 10 minutes of duck cooking put dressing on salad. 6. Leave mango in refrigerator until last minute.

MENU 9   CHICKEN DINNER

	Method	Heat & Time on Barbecue	Work Plan
Smooth Spinach Soup (p 190)	Conventional hob		Cook soup 24 hours ahead but do not add cream or lemon juice.
Roast Herby Chicken (p 90)	Spit	Medium 2½–3 hours	Several hours ahead make sure frozen chicken (if to be used) is completely thawed; mix seasonings and margarine, spread inside chicken and truss, refrigerate; have skewer, spit and dips ready.
Plain Boiled Rice (p 183)	Conventional hob		Cook rice early if preferred, and leave ready for reheating.
Fruit and Roasted-peanut Salad with Orange Dressing (p 166)	Kitchen preparation		Ahead of time prepare and mix lettuce, celery, radishes, spring onions, green peppers and peanuts; do *not* prepare apple.
Lemon Mousse (p 201)	Kitchen preparation		Up to 24 hours ahead prepare and refrigerate.

Cooking Count-Down 1. Light coals. 2. Thread chicken on spit and set to cook. 3. Reheat soup. 4. Cook or reheat rice and keep hot. 5. Prepare apple and finish salad. 6. Stir cream and lemon into soup just before serving. 7. Serve soup when chicken is almost cooked. 8. Serve mousse last.

MENU 10

FRENCH PROVENÇAL DINNER

	Method	Heat & Time on Barbecue	Work Plan
Lettuce Soup (p 192)	Conventional hob		If soup is being served hot, prepare ingredients ahead of time up to liquidizer stage but do not complete cooking.
Seafood Brochettes (p 125)	Skewers	Hot 4 minutes	Several hours ahead marinate the seafood; prepare béarnaise sauce; slice lemon; put butter in foil dish.
Brochettes de Boeuf (p 124)	Skewers on grid	Medium 20 minutes	2 hours ahead marinate meat; prepare vegetables.
Green Salad	Kitchen preparation		Ahead of time wash salad and arrange in bowl; cover and keep cool.
Boiled Rice (p 183)	Conventional hob		Cook the rice early as you will have too much to do later to consider last-minute cooking.
Pineapple Rings with Kirsch (p 208)	Kitchen preparation		A few hours ahead slice pineapple and sprinkle with kirsch and sugar; set aside on non-stick paper; get cherries ready and chop angelica; get out frying pan and put butter in dish.

Cooking Count-Down 1. Light coals. 2. Skewer seafood. 3. Skewer meat. 4. Have oil ready for basting meat. 5. Put béarnaise sauce in dish. 6. Complete soup. 7. Serve soup. 8. Clear dishes and put rice to reheat in kitchen. 9. Put seafood brochettes to cook. 10. Put beef to cook while eating seafood. 11. Bring rice to barbecue. 12. Bring out salad. 13. Cook and serve pineapple.

MENU 11

PORK DINNER

	Method	Heat & Time on Barbecue	Work Plan
Pasta Salad (p 172)	Kitchen preparation		Prepare up to 1 day ahead.
Spit-roast Pork with Apple Sauce (p 90)	Spit	Low 1½ hours	Cook apple sauce up to 1 day ahead and put in saucepan a few hours ahead; cover; have foil dish ready.
Glazed Sweet Potatoes (p 180)	Conventional hob		1–2 hours ahead prepare and put in casserole.
Rumtopf (p 199)	Kitchen preparation		Prepare 1–3 months ahead.

Cooking Count-Down 1. Light coals. 2. Put potatoes to cook in conventional oven. 3. Put roast on spit. 4. About ½ hour before roast is ready, reheat apple sauce. 5. Serve salad. 6. Bring sauce to barbecue. 7. Bring potatoes to barbecue. 8. Serve rumtopf.

AMERICAN DINNER

MENU 12

	Method	Heat & Time on Barbecue	Work Plan
Curried Seafood Cocktail (p 139)	Kitchen preparation		1 hour ahead of time make curried mayonnaise; wash and dry lettuce; shred lettuce and put in glasses; cover and keep cool.
Texan Hotsup Drumsticks (p 100)	Foil on grid	Medium 30–40 minutes	Prepare sauce 3 hours ahead; wrap up drumsticks 1 hour ahead.
Corn Fritters (p 182)	Kitchen preparation		Cook and drain corn several hours ahead; make batter and mix together; cover and leave at room temperature.
Bacon-Rolled Sausages (p 77)	Grid	Medium 20 minutes	Wrap bacon round sausages several hours ahead.
Whole Tomatoes in Foil (p 103)	Foil on grid	Medium 10 minutes	Wrap tomatoes in foil several hours ahead.
Peaches with Grand Marnier Flambé (p 113)	Fry	Hot 5 minutes	2 hours ahead skin peaches; gather remaining ingredients and frying pan.

Cooking Count-Down 1. Light coals. 2. Assemble seafood cocktail. 3. Cook fritters and keep hot in oven. 4. Set drumsticks to cook. 5. Serve seafood cocktail. 6. Set sausages to cook. 7. Bring fritters to barbecue. 8. Cook tomatoes. 9. Cook peaches.

MENU 13

VEGETARIAN DINNER

	Method	Heat & Time on Barbecue	Work Plan
Three-bean Soup (p 191)	Conventional hob		Prepare up to 2 days ahead and refrigerate; get out suitable heavy-based tureen.
Nutburgers (p 109)	Fry	Medium or High 10 mins	Prepare and shape up to 24 hours ahead.
Easy Baked Aubergine with Fondue Sauce (p 99)	Foil in coals	Medium 30 mins	1 hour ahead of time prepare and wrap aubergines; gather ingredients for fondue. Set out board for cutting aubergines.
Rice and Sultana Salad (p 169)	Kitchen preparation		Several hours ahead prepare and stuff tomatoes.
Green Salad	Kitchen preparation		Shred lettuce, cover and refrigerate.
Melon Basket (p 204)	Kitchen preparation		Several hours ahead prepare baskets.

Cooking Count-Down 1. Light coals. 2. Collect frying pan and oil if burgers are being fried. 3. Prepare fondue sauce in foil dish. 4. Put soup to reheat. 5. Put aubergine in coals. 6. Serve soup while cooking Nutburgers. 7. Serve salad. 8. Reheat and attend to fondue sauce. 9. Retrieve aubergines from foil and cut on board. 10. Spread aubergines with sauce and serve with green salad. 11. Serve melon.

MENU 14   INDIAN DINNER

	Method	Heat & Time on Barbecue	Work Plan
Punjabi Curry Soup (p 194)	Conventional hob		Make 12 hours ahead and chill; have soup bowls ready.
Tandoori Chicken (p 82)	Grid	Medium 25–35 minutes	Marinate at least 24 hours ahead.
Vegetable Pilau (p 185)	Conventional hob		Cook well ahead and refrigerate or freeze if a microwave oven is available for reheating, otherwise cook a few hours ahead up to frying nuts stage.
Aloo Kebabs (p 122)	Skewers on grid	Hot 10–12 minutes	Boil potatoes a few hours earlier, thread and brush with curry paste; wrap in clingfilm.
Nan (p 136)	Kitchen preparation		Pre-cook and keep wrapped; or purchase.
Raita (p 146)			Prepare up to 6 hours ahead and refrigerate.
Gulabjamun (p 206)	Conventional hob		Prepare 1 or 2 days ahead and refrigerate.

Cooking Count-Down 1. Light coals. 2. Finish cooking pilau. 3. Remove chicken from marinade and put remaining marinade in dish; have brush ready. 4. Bring Nan and Raita to barbecue. 5. Cover hot rice with foil and bring to barbecue. 6. Put chicken to cook. 7. Serve soup. 8. Put Aloo Kebabs to cook. 9. Briefly heat Nan on sides of barbecue. 10. Bring dessert from refrigerator.

MENU 15   MIDDLE EASTERN DINNER

	Method	Heat & Time on Barbecue	Work Plan
Dolmades (p 186)	Kitchen preparation		Prepare up to 2 days ahead and serve cold.
Middle Eastern Kofta (p 109) or Keftedhes Aya Naba (p 112)	Fry	Medium 8–10 minutes	If serving Kofta prepare and shape several hours ahead into balls. If serving Aya Naba prepare and shape several hours ahead (the two recipes have similarities and if you are preparing both, mince the lamb and onion together, then divide the mixture and add other ingredients for each recipe).
Skewered Chicken and Green Peppers (p 127)	Skewers on grid	Medium 20 minutes	Prepare the chicken and other ingredients several hours ahead; thread on skewers and brush with marinade and leave in refrigerator until required.
Marinated Cucumber Salad (p 170)	Kitchen preparation		Prepare 4 hours ahead.
Aubergine Salad (p 168)	Kitchen preparation		Make 12 hours ahead.
Spring Onion and Lettuce Salad	Kitchen preparation		Prepare 2 or 3 hours earlier and keep in covered salad bowl in refrigerator.

(Menu 15 continued overleaf)

(Menu 15 continued)

	Method	Heat & Time on Barbecue	Work Plan
Pitta Bread	Kitchen preparation		Buy fresh or frozen.
Baklava (p 205)	Conventional oven		Make up to 3 days ahead or purchase from specialist shop if you feel lazy.

Cooking Count-Down 1. Light coals. 2. Bring all food except Baklava out to barbecue. 3. Put chicken skewers to cook. 4. Serve Dolmades. 5. Put Kofta or Keftedhes to cook. 6. Heat pitta on sides of barbecue. 7. Serve Baklava at end of meal.

MENU 16   JAPANESE DINNER

	Method	Heat & Time on Barbecue	Work Plan
Matsutake Soup (p 189)	Conventional hob		Prepare ingredients ahead of time and cook up to skim stage; leave in saucepan.
Lemon Sole with Miso Paste (p 81)	Grid	Medium 3 minutes	Prepare and spread with miso paste, cover and refrigerate.
Crispy Spinach Rolls (p 75)	Grid	Medium 5–10 minutes	Cook, shape and refrigerate.
Prawn and Chicken Stuffed Aubergine (p 97)	Foil in coals	Medium 35–40 minutes	Several hours ahead cook filling, stuff aubergines and wrap; refrigerate.
Plain Boiled Rice (p 183)	Conventional hob		Pre-cook if preferred.
Sliced Spring Onions	Kitchen preparation		Several hours ahead slice thinly and put on serving dish; cover tightly.

Cooking Count-Down 1. Light coals. 2. Put fish in baskets. 3. Have extra miso paste in dish. 4. Put aubergine in coals. 5. Cook or reheat rice. 6. Complete soup and bring to barbecue. 7. Put fish to cook while eating soup. 8. Serve fish and onions. 9. Bring rice to barbecue. 10. Lift grid and serve aubergine, rice.

MENU 17   CHINESE DINNER

	Method	Heat & Time on Barbecue	Work Plan
Chinatown Soup (p 189)	Conventional hob		1 hour ahead cook soup up to 'noodle' stage in saucepan or suitable metal tureen; switch off heat and cover.
Prawn Crackers	Conventional hob		Cook in hot oil several hours ahead.
Lobster tails With Sesame Seeds (p 74)	Grid	25 minutes on side	¾ hour ahead prepare lobster tails and marinate.
Malaysian Satay in Peanut Sauce (p 128)	Skewers on grid	Hot 10 minutes	A few hours ahead prepare and marinate; prepare cucumber and salt.
Fried Egg Rice (p 184) or Boiled Rice (p 183)	Conventional hob		A few hours ahead cook rice; make up egg mixture.
Oriental Salad (p 165)	Kitchen preparation		1½ hours ahead wash, drain and dry beansprouts; prepare other ingredients and put in salad bowl.
Sliced Oranges in Ginger Syrup (p 207)	Kitchen preparation		Prepare several hours ahead and chill.

Cooking Count-Down 1. Light coals. 2. Thread meat, fish and chicken on skewers. 3. Coat skewers with marinade and pour remainder into foil basin. 4. Cook egg mixture and slice. 5. Reheat rice and mix in egg and bring to barbecue. 6. Finish salad. 7. Put lobster tails to cook. 8. Reheat soup, add noodles and simmer for 5 minutes, then bring to barbecue with prawn crackers. 9. Put satay on to cook. 10. Serve oranges in ginger syrup at end of meal.

	Method	Heat & Time on Barbecue	Work Plan
Sangria (p 214)	Kitchen preparation		Prepare 4 hours ahead and chill but do not add soda and ice.
Guacamole (p 143)	Kitchen preparation		Prepare up to 4 hours ahead; cover and chill; serve while kebabs are cooking.
Nacho Chips (available from delicatessens)			Open packets just before serving.
Mexiburgers (p 76)	Grid	Medium 8–10 minutes	Prepare and shape up to 24 hours ahead.
Taos Kebabs (p 123)	Skewers on grid	Medium 20 minutes	Prepare and marinate several hours ahead.
Chilli Sauce (p 134)	Kitchen preparation		Prepare up to 2 days ahead; bring hot from kitchen and put beside barbecue; no matter if it goes cold.
Tortillas (p 135)			Store pre-cooked tortillas in refrigerator or freezer; bring back to room temperature one hour ahead.
Fruit Platter with Tequila Dip (p 145)	Kitchen preparation		Prepare dip up to 24 hours ahead; prepare fruit several hours ahead and refrigerate.

Cooking Count-Down 1. Light barbecue. 2. Thread kebabs. 3. Add soda and ice to sangria and serve. 4. Open nacho chips and put in bowl. 5. Bring out guacamole. 6. Put chilli sauce in foil dish, cover and bring to barbecue to reheat which can be done while coals are 'taking'. 7. Set kebabs to cook. 8. Put burgers to cook. 9. Reheat tortillas just before serving. 10. Serve fruit platter and dip.

MENU 19   ROMANTIC DINNER FOR TWO

	Method	Heat & Time on Barbecue	Work Plan
Champagne			Chill ahead of time.
Louisiana Seafood Dip (p 147) (⅓ recipe)	Conventional hob		A few hours ahead of time gather ingredients and cook soup, mushrooms, onions, herbs and spices in metal casserole; cover with lid.
French Bread			
Grilled Lobster (p 84)	Grid	Medium 15 minutes	A few hours ahead of time cook lobster, halve and remove sac; make seasoned butter and spread on lobster halves; refrigerate.
Green Salad	Kitchen preparation		Ahead of time wash salad and arrange in bowl; cover and keep cool.
Salad Kebabs (p 171) (⅓ recipe)	Kitchen preparation		A few hours ahead make dressing; prepare and marinate vegetables.
Strawberry Syllabub (p 200) (¼ recipe)	Kitchen preparation		Several hours ahead make syllabub and put into individual glasses; slice strawberries, put on a plate and refrigerate.
Dinner Mints			
Coffee			

(Menu 19 continued overleaf)

(Menu 19 continued)

Cooking Count-Down 1. Put champagne on ice. 2. Light coals. 3. Thread vegetables on skewers and bring to barbecue. 4. Decorate syllabubs. 5. Prepare percolator for coffee. 6. Cut French bread and bring to barbecue. 7. Complete seafood dip and bring to barbecue. 8. Bring lobster to barbecue with extra butter in dish; also lobster crackers and pick; finger bowl containing water and slice of lemon; and two clean white napkins. 9. Bring green salad and salad kebabs to barbecue. 10. Take champagne off ice. 11. Serve Louisiana dip while cooking lobster. 12. Serve lobster and salads. 13. Bring syllabubs from refrigerator and put coffee on to brew.

MENU 20   **KEBAB MEAL**

	Method	Heat & Time on Barbecue	Work Plan
Foil-baked Stuffed Edam Cheese (p 103)	Foil on grid	Medium 15–20 minutes	Several hours ahead prepare and stuff the cheese and wrap in foil.
Gammon and Green Pepper Kebabs with Tomato and Honey Sauce (p 121)	Skewers on grid	Medium 10 minutes	Several hours ahead of time marinate the gammon and green peppers.
Kidney Kebabs (p 126)	Skewers on grid	Hot 4–5 minutes	2 hours ahead of time thread kidneys on to skewers; put butter in foil dish.
Mustard Butter (p 151)	Kitchen preparation		Prepare several days ahead; also shape and cut into pats and freeze on non-stick paper if preferred.
Chicken and Grapefruit Kebabs (p 127)	Skewers on grid	Medium 15 minutes	Several hours ahead prepare and marinate chicken; segment grapefruit; cut gammon into strips.
Almond, Sesame Seed and Carrot Noodles (p 178)	Grid or conventional oven	Medium 10 minutes	1½ hours ahead prepare up to noodle stage.

(Menu 20 continued overleaf)

(Menu 20 continued)

	Method	Heat & Time on Barbecue	Work Plan
Green Salad	Kitchen preparation		Prepare green salad without dressing a few hours ahead.
Waldorf Salad (p 167)	Kitchen preparation		Prepare and garnish a few hours ahead.
Brandied Five-fruit Kebabs (p 122)	Skewers on grid	Medium 6–7 minutes	One hour ahead prepare fruit; prepare sauce and brush fruit with sauce; put remaining sauce in dish and have brush ready.

Cooking Count-Down 1. Light coals. 2. Thread gammon and green peppers on to skewers. 3. Cook sauce and put into basin on side of grill. 4. Thread chicken and grapefruit on to skewers and sprinkle with paprika. 5. Take marinade to barbecue and have brush ready. 6. Cook cheese. 7. Preheat oven to bake noodles. 8. Put gammon and chicken kebabs to cook. 9. Put noodles in conventional oven. 10. Serve cheese. 11. Put kidney kebabs to cook. 12. Serve kebabs, noodles and salads. 13. Cook fruit kebabs at end of meal.

5
Grilling

Guide for Grilling
Lobster Tails with Sesame Seeds
Crispy Spinach Rolls
Lamb Chop Medley
Mexiburgers
Pork Chops in Cider and Clove Butter
Bacon-rolled Sausages
Hovis Turkey Loaves
Pork Chops with Apricot Stuffing
Trout with Sorrel Sauce
Beef, Cheese and Pickle Burgers
Lemon Sole with Miso Paste
Tandoori Chicken
Korean Sliced Beef
Grilled Lobster
Grilled Salmon Steaks
Mini Roasts

GUIDE FOR GRILLING

Food	Time	Coals
BEEF		
Joint	2–3 hours	LOW
Steaks (2.5 cm/1 in)		
Rare	10 minutes	HOT
Medium	15 minutes	HOT
Well done	20 minutes	HOT
BURGERS (1–1.8 cm/½–¾ in)		
Medium	8–10 minutes	Thin HOT,
Well done	15 minutes	Thick MEDIUM
FISH, Steaks and		
Cutlets (1.8 cm/¾ in)	15 minutes	MEDIUM
KEBABS	20 minutes	MEDIUM
LAMB		
Leg joint	2½ hours	LOW
Chops	15–20 minutes	MEDIUM
PORK		
Joint with bone	15–20 minutes per lb	LOW
Joint without bone	20–25 minutes per lb	LOW
Chops	30–40 minutes	MEDIUM
Spare rib chops	1–1¼ hours	LOW

Food	Time	Coals
POULTRY		
Whole chicken		
(1.8 kg/3½ lb)	1½–2 hours	MEDIUM
Whole duck	1½–2 hours	MEDIUM
Turkey	1½–2½ hours	MEDIUM
plus 15 minutes standing time		
Drumsticks and thighs	20–25 minutes	MEDIUM
SAUSAGES		
Beef	15 minutes	MEDIUM
Pork	20 minutes	MEDIUM
Frankfurters	5–10 minutes	MEDIUM
Cocktail sausages	5 minutes	MEDIUM
Sausage meat	10 minutes	MEDIUM
	(depending on thickness)	

Lobster Tails with Sesame Seeds

   6 lobster tails
   Salt
   Monosodium glutamate (optional)
   45 ml (3 tbsp) dry sherry
   30 ml (2 tbsp) vegetable oil
   10 ml (2 tsp) soy sauce
   15 ml (1 tbsp) lemon juice
   10 ml (2 tsp) toasted sesame seeds

Remove the soft shell from the lobster tails. Combine the remaining ingredients in a bowl. Put in the lobster tails and turn over two or three times so that they are well basted. Leave to stand for 15 minutes.

Cook the lobster tails flesh-side up on the side of the grid or on the grid over indirect coals for 10 minutes, then baste and cook for a further 10 minutes. Turn the lobster tails over and cook for a further 5 minutes.

Serves 6, but the quantities may be increased.

Crispy Spinach Rolls

4 eggs
5 ml (1 tsp) salt
30 ml (2 tbsp) light soy sauce
15 ml (1 tbsp) milk
10 ml (2 level tsp) plain flour
butter for frying
450 g (1 lb) fresh spinach, washed and with stems removed

Beat the eggs, salt, soy sauce, milk and flour together to make a batter. Make ten wafer-thin 15 cm (6 in) omelettes, browning them on one side only.

Cook the spinach lightly, then press out all the liquid. Chop the spinach, seasoning with salt and pepper. Place a spoonful of spinach on one edge of each pancake and roll up, tucking in the sides after the first fold, then completing the rolling.

Cook on the side of the grid for 5–10 minutes or on a foil tray in the centre of the grid.

Serves 6–12, but the recipe can be increased.

Lamb Chop Medley

18 lamb cutlets 2.5 cm (1 in) thick
Mango chutney
French mustard
Dried or fresh sprigs rosemary

Trim any excess fat from the chops and scrape the flesh away from the tip of the bone. Using a sharp knife cut horizontally through the eye of the chop as far as the bone. Fill the cavities of six of the chops with the mango chutney, six with mustard and the remaining six with the herbs.

Grill the chops, pressing them flat against the grid with a fish slice. Turn the chops over as soon as the first side is browned and complete the cooking towards the sides of the grid.

Serves 6, but the quantities can be increased.

Mexiburgers

   800 g (2 lb) lean beef
   200 g (8 oz) lean ham
   100 g (4 oz) salami, skinned
   2 heaped tbsp kidney beans, freshly cooked or canned, drained
   1 medium onion, skinned
   1 small green pepper, seeded
   75 ml (5 tbsp) tomato purée
   5 ml (1 level tsp) chilli powder
   Salt and pepper
   1 egg, beaten

Finely mince together the beef, ham, salami, kidney beans, onion and green pepper. Put into a mixing bowl and add the remaining ingredients. Mix thoroughly then shape into 1 cm (½ in) thick burgers.

Brush the grid with oil and grill the burgers over medium coals, turning them once after about 2 minutes. Allow a total of 8–10 minutes' cooking time.

Makes about 20, but surplus uncooked burgers can be frozen. Left-over cooked burgers can be easily reheated in the microwave oven.

Pork Chops in Cider and Clove Butter

6 pork chops, trimmed
300 ml (½ pt) dry cider
5 ml (1 level tsp) ground cloves
100 g (4 oz) butter
2.5 ml (½ tsp) salt
2.5 ml (½ tsp) pepper

Prick the chops thoroughly and soak in the cider for 2 hours, turning occasionally.

Cream the cloves, butter and seasonings together in a foil dish.

Put the cider marinade in a small saucepan, bring to the boil and cook rapidly until only 4 tablespoons of the cider remain. Spoon the reduced marinade over the chops, then spread on both sides with the creamed butter mixture.

Grill over medium coals for about 30 minutes or until the internal temperature of the chops is 75°C (170°F). Barely melt the remaining clove butter in the dish on the side of the grid and baste the chops twice during cooking.

Serves 6, but the recipe can be increased.

Bacon-rolled Sausages

One de-rinded rasher streaky bacon per sausage
Large unpricked sausages

Lay the bacon rashers on a board or work surface and stretch each one separately with the back of a table knife. Coil a bacon rasher round each sausage and grill for 20 minutes over medium coals, turning the sausages frequently. For the best results start with the short edge of bacon underneath.

BACON ROLLED SAUSAGE

Hovis Turkey Loaves

800 g (2 lb) minced raw turkey meat
100 g (4 oz) fresh Hovis breadcrumbs
1 small onion, finely chopped
1 level tsp dried marjoram
1 tsp French mustard
1 tsp Worcestershire sauce
3 tbsp milk
Salt
Pepper
2 eggs, beaten

For basting

100 g (4 oz) butter
6 tbsp tomato paste

Mix the ingredients (except those for basting) together
and form into six Hovis shapes. Refrigerate for half an
hour to stiffen the mixture.

Meanwhile put the butter and tomato paste into a small
pan and heat, stirring until the mixture blends.

Brush each loaf all over with the tomato mixture and
cook on the grid over medium coals for 45–60 minutes
turning the turkey loaves over on to all sides and basting
frequently with the tomato sauce.

Serves 6, but the recipe can be increased.

Pork Chops with Apricot Stuffing

6 thick pork chops

For the stuffing
100 g (4 oz) dried apricots
1 small onion, skinned and finely chopped
25 g (1 oz) butter
65 g (2½ oz) fresh white breadcrumbs
1 tbsp lemon juice
1 level tsp dried rosemary leaves
1 level tsp dry mustard
Salt
Pepper

First make the stuffing. Put the apricots in a saucepan, just cover with cold water, then bring to the boil and simmer for 5 minutes. Drain the apricots and roughly chop.

Fry the onion in the butter until soft, then remove the pan from the heat and stir in the apricots and the remaining ingredients, seasoning to taste with salt and pepper. The mixture should be fairly stiff.

Trim all the fat from the chops and cut horizontally through the centre of the chop towards the bone to form a pocket – do *not* cut the chop completely in half. Divide the stuffing into six portions and press one into the centre pocket of each chop.

Reshape the chops and secure with skewers so that the stuffing does not fall out. Cook on the oiled grid over medium or low coals for 25–30 minutes, turning the chops half-way through cooking.

Serves 6, but the recipe can be increased.

Trout with Sorrel Sauce

    6 trout, washed and dried
    Melted butter, or oil
    Foil

For the sorrel sauce
    40 g (1½ oz) butter
    100 g (4 oz) fresh sorrel leaves
    300 ml (½ pt) single cream
    25 g (1 oz) curd cheese, well beaten with salt and pepper

First make the sauce. To do this, put the butter into a saucepan and heat until foamy then stir in the sorrel and cook for 1–2 minutes until the leaves are soft. Add the cream, then remove the pan from the heat and beat in the seasoned curd cheese. Blend in the liquidizer and pour into a sauce boat.

Before preparing the fish fold a 30 cm (12 in) length of aluminium foil in half. Cut into two lengths 7.5 cm (3 in) wide and then fold over to make thin bracelets.

Brush the fish with the oil or melted butter, then wrap one of the bracelets near the head end and one in the centre of the fish, folding over any surplus to form a hook.

Cook the fish over medium coals – preferably in a covered grill, otherwise tented with foil – and turn over the fish once during cooking and brush frequently with the melted butter or oil. Use the foil loops to help you turn the fish over carefully.

Allow about 20 minutes' cooking time.

The fish is cooked when the juices run clear and the flesh can be flaked easily with a fork. Serve with the cooled sorrel sauce.

Serves 6, but the recipe can be increased.

Note: Frozen or dried sorrel can be used if fresh sorrel is not available. Take care that the moisture in the frozen sorrel does not cause the foaming butter to spit. If using dried herbs allow a little more cooking time.

Beef, Cheese and Pickle Burgers

900 g (2 lb) raw minced beef
175 g (6 oz) Edam cheese, grated
2 eggs, beaten
4 heaped dsp Branston pickle
1 level tsp dried oregano
Golden breadcrumbs

Thoroughly mix the beef, cheese, eggs, pickle and oregano together (the mixture will be soft). Shape into six or eight 1 cm (½ in) thick burgers and sprinkle with the golden crumbs, then turn the burgers over with a fish slice and sprinkle golden crumbs on the other side. Refrigerate for half an hour to firm the burgers.

Oil the grid and cook over medium coals for about 15–20 minutes, turning the burgers over half-way through cooking. Serve in soft bread rolls.

Serves 6–8, but the recipe can be increased.

Lemon Sole with Miso Paste

90 ml (6 tbsp) red bean paste (Miso available from health shops)
15 ml (1 tbsp) granulated sugar
45 ml (3 tbsp) sweet white wine
25 g (1 oz) butter
3 large lemon sole

For serving

1 bunch spring onions, peeled and diagonally sliced, paper thin

Combine the Miso (red bean) paste, sugar and wine in small saucepan and cook over gentle heat until thick. Sti in the butter, then remove from the heat.

Cut the fish in half lengthwise and then halve each piec crosswise. Using a sharp knife make a pocket on eithe side of the bone. Brush with the sauce both on the insid and the outside of the fish.

Arrange the fish in a single layer in a hinged fish gri basket and close the sides, then grill on each side for minutes or until the fish is cooked. Brush again with th sauce towards the end of the cooking time.

Serve with a salad of freshly sliced spring onions.

Serves 6, but the recipe can be increased.

Tandoori Chicken

60 ml (4 level tbsp) tandoori powder mixture
150 ml (¼ pt) natural yogurt
30 ml (2 tbsp) lemon juice
5 ml (1 tsp) salt
1 × 1.4–1.8 kg (3–3½ lb) chicken breasts on the bone

Mix together the tandoori powder, yogurt, lemon juic and salt in a large mixing bowl. Slash the chicken piece through the skin as far as the bone in two or three place and fill the slits with the tandoori mixture. Now put th chicken pieces into the tandoori paste in the mixing bow and turn them over, basting well, until they are a thoroughly coated. Cover and leave for 12–24 hours turning and basting three or four times.

Brush the grid with vegetable oil and cook the chicke pieces skin-sides down in a covered barbecue over mediun coals for 25–35 minutes, turning three or four times durin cooking. Basting during cooking is not necessary.

Serves 6, but the recipe can be increased.

Note: Tandoori powder is obtainable from Indian-type shops or you can order it from the Curry Club in Haslemere, Surrey. However, you can make it yourself.

Combine 1 tsp each of ground cardamom and cinnamon, 2 tsp each of chilli compound powder, ground cumin, ground ginger, with 4 tsp ground coriander. Finally add ¼ tsp each of ground cloves and black pepper, and a little red food colouring powder. (If you find that red food colouring powder is not widely available, substitute a few drops of liquid food colouring.)

Korean Sliced Beef

    450 g (1 lb) topside of beef
    ¼ tsp monosodium glutamate
    ¼ tsp garlic salt
    1 tsp sesame oil
    6 spring onions, skinned and finely chopped

Slice the meat thinly across the grain. Combine all the other ingredients in a large bowl. Add the meat and stir until it is well coated, then cover and leave to marinate for at least 1 hour, stirring occasionally.

Cook the meat strips over hot coals on a well-oiled grid for 1–2 minutes only, turning the strips over once during cooking.

Serves 4, but the recipe can be increased.

Grilled Lobster

    1 × 900 g (2 lb) lobster, freshly boiled
    50 g (2 oz) butter
    Salt
    1 tbsp freshly chopped parsley
    1 spring onion, peeled and finely chopped
    2 capers, finely chopped

Halve the lobster and remove the sac. Melt the butter, season with salt and add the parsley, onion and capers. Brush the flesh-side of the lobster with the prepared butter.

Brush the grid with oil and cook the lobster shell-side down over medium coals for about 10 minutes. Brush the cut sides of the lobster with the seasoned butter, turn flesh-side down and cook for a further 5 minutes or until the flesh is opaque.

Serve each half-lobster on a plate with additional melted butter and have lobster crackers and a skewer to hand so that you can enjoy every last piece of this delicious seafood.

Serves 2, but the recipe can be increased.

Note: You can now buy frozen cooked lobster but this should be thawed before splitting and cooking.

Grilled Salmon Steaks

6 × 175 g (6 oz) salmon steaks
Salt
Pepper
100 g (4 oz) butter, melted
Garlic sauce (see page 137)

Rinse and dry the salmon steaks, then season with salt and pepper and brush with melted butter.

Cook the steaks on the grid for 8–10 minutes over hot coals, turning them over half-way through the cooking period.

Serves 6, but the recipe can be increased according to the amount of space you have on the barbecue.

Mini Roasts

Although this recipe is most suitable for beef, it can be used for lamb, veal or pork which will take a little longer to cook.

2 × 900 g (2 lb) rolled joints topside of beef, each measuring 10–12.5 cm (4–5 in) in diameter.
Oil for brushing

Untie each joint and cut in half lengthwise so that you have four long pieces 5–6 cm (2–2½ in) in diameter when rolled. Replace the fat along one side of each joint, roll up and tie securely with the string. To do this easily, take a long piece of string and tie a loop at one end. Wrap the string round one end of the beef, pulling the straight end through the loop. Pull the string to about 1.25 cm (½ in) above the first tie and loop through, pulling tightly. Repeat until you have five or six rings of string tied along the joint. Tie securely at the end.

Brush the joints with oil and place on the grid over hot coals. Cook for about 20 minutes, turning the joints frequently.

Serves 8–12, but the recipe can be increased but cooking time remains the same.

6

Spit Roasting

Spit-roast Duck with Deep South Sauce
Roast Herby Chicken
Spit-roast Pork with Apple Sauce
Spit-roast Chicken with Rhubarb Sauce
Roast Leg of Lamb Nogal

Spit-roast Duck with Deep South Sauce

1 × 2.75 kg (6 lb) duckling
Grated rind and juice of 2 large oranges
150 ml (¼ pt) sweet red wine
4 tbsp clear honey
25 g (½ oz) butter
White part of 3 or 4 spring onions, finely sliced
Salt
Pepper

Prick the duck through the skin in several places, then fix on to the spit. Place a roasting or foil dish into the hot coals underneath the duck to catch the fat.

Cook the bird over medium indirect heat for 2–3 hours or until the meat thermometer registers 85°C (185°F).

Meanwhile combine all the remaining ingredients together in a saucepan and bring to the boil. Season with salt and pepper and simmer the mixture without covering for about 30 minutes or until the sauce is thick and syrupy. Remove from the heat.

Start basting the duck with the sauce half-way through its spit-roasting time and continue to baste every 10 minutes.

Serves 6–8, but the recipe can be increased if you have room for two ducks on the spit.

Roast Herby Chicken

　1 × 1.8 kg (4 lb) oven-ready chicken

For the seasoning
　2 celery stalks
　1 medium onion
　1 level tsp salt
　¼ level tsp freshly ground black pepper
　Juice and pulp of 1 lemon
　2 heaped tbsp freshly chopped parsley
　1 level tbsp fresh lemon thyme leaves
　1 level tsp dark soft brown sugar
　25 g (1 oz) soft margarine

Mince the celery and onion together, then combine in a bowl with the remainder of the seasoning ingredients. Spread the mixture round the inside of the cavity. Skewer the chicken, paying particular attention to the neck end to prevent the seasoning from falling out, then thoroughly prick the skin all over.

　Fix the chicken on to the spit, put a roasting or foil dish into the coals to catch the fat, and cook over medium indirect heat for 2½–3 hours. For best results tent the bird with a foil hood, making an opening at either end for the spit handles to turn.

Serves 6, but two or three birds can be threaded on to the barbecue at the same time. Increase the other ingredients accordingly.

Spit-roast Pork with Apple Sauce

　1 × 1.4 kg (3 lb) shoulder of pork, boned and rolled

Apple sauce
　450 g (1 lb) cooking apples
　15 g (½ oz) butter

Juice and rind of ½ lemon
50 g (2 oz) caster sugar

Fix the pork joint on the spit, securing it centrally. Set a roasting or foil dish into low coals to catch the fat.

Cook the meat for about 1½ hours or until the internal temperature of the joint registers 75°C (170°F). Leave to rest for 10–15 minutes before carving.

To make the apple sauce, peel, core and slice the apples and place in a heavy-based saucepan with the butter, lemon juice and rind, adding 30 ml (2 tbsp) water. Cover and cook gently until the apples are pulped. Beat well until smooth, then beat in the sugar. (Although the apple sauce can be cooked over the barbecue, it is not possible to do this while the spit is in position. Either precook the sauce on the barbecue or cook on the conventional hob.)

Pour the sauce into a heavy-foil bowl, cover and keep hot on the side of the barbecue.

Serves 8, but the recipe can be increased, without adding extra time if two joints are threaded on the same spit.

Spit-roast Chicken with Rhubarb Sauce

2 × 1.4 kg (3½ lb) oven-ready roasting chicken

Rhubarb sauce
450 g (1 lb) rhubarb, washed and finely chopped
50–75 g (2–3 oz) soft dark brown sugar
150 ml (¼ pt) cider
1 tsp lemon juice
½ level tsp ground nutmeg

Thread the chicken on to the spit (placing a roasting or foil dish in the coals to catch the fat) and cook over indirect medium heat for 1½–2 hours or until the internal temperature of the poultry reaches 85°C (180°F).

To make the sauce put all the ingredients into a heavy-based pan and cook over gentle heat, stirring frequently, until the mixture is soft and pulpy. Pour the sauce into a flame-proof or double-thickness-foil bowl, cover and keep hot on the side of the barbecue.

Serve the chicken sliced or jointed, coated with the sauce.

Serves 12, but the recipe can be halved.

Roast Leg of Lamb Nogal

An expensive but luxurious special occasion dish.

    1 whole leg of lamb
    50 g (2 oz) lard or white cooking fat
    450 g (1 lb) carrots, peeled and chopped
    3 onions, skinned and chopped
    2 cloves garlic, skinned and crushed
    2 wineglasses red wine
    1 wineglass brandy
    Few sprigs fresh marjoram
    Few sprigs fresh rosemary
    1 tsp salt
    ½ tsp pepper
    1 wineglass dry sherry

To garnish
    Sprigs fresh marjoram and rosemary
    2 tbsp brandy

Insert the spit along the bone of the leg of lamb, fixing the clamps securely to either end. Cook on a covered grill over a roasting or foil dish set in medium coals for 1¼–1½ hours or until the internal temperature of the meat is 65°C (145°F).

Melt the lard in a heavy-based saucepan and stir in the

carrots, onions, garlic, wine, brandy, herbs and seasonings. Cook, covered, until the carrots and onions are soft enough to mash. Purée the sauce mixture in the liquidizer or press through a sieve. Stir in the sherry, then pour the mixture into a double-thickness-foil dish or suitable metal pan and keep hot on the side of the barbecue.

From time to time baste the meat with the sauce. When the lamb is cooked, place it on a serving dish, pierce the skin with a sharp knife and implant sprigs of marjoram and rosemary so that they stand upright. Warm the brandy in a metal ladle over the barbecue and pour over the lamb and ignite the herbs. Serve the sauce separately.

Serves 8–12, depending on the size of the lamb joint.

7
Foil Cookery

Prawn and Chicken Stuffed Aubergine
Chocolate-stuffed Bananas with Crème de Cacao
Honey Bananas
Rolled Escalopes of Veal with Almonds and Cinzano
  Bianco
Easy Baked Aubergine with Fondue Sauce
Texan Hotsup Drumsticks
Triple Lamb Chops en Papillote
Hungarian Lamb Chops
Foil-baked Corn on the Cob
Whole Tomatoes in Foil
Foil-baked Stuffed Edam Cheese
Barbecued Garlic Bread
Jacket Potatoes

Prawn and Chicken Stuffed Aubergine

6 small aubergines
25 g (1 oz) butter
1 large onion, finely chopped
1 clove garlic, crushed
6–8 tomatoes, skinned and chopped
75 g (3 oz) cooked chicken
75 g (3 oz) cooked shelled prawns
15 ml (1 tbsp) soy sauce
2.5 ml (½ tsp) grated ginger root
Salt
Pepper

Halve the aubergines lengthwise and scoop out the flesh leaving a thin wall. Chop the flesh finely.

Melt the butter in a saucepan, add the chopped aubergine, the onions and garlic. Sauté gently until the aubergine is tender. Stir in the remaining ingredients and season to taste with salt and pepper.

Fill the aubergine shells with the mixture, pressing it well down, then flat wrap in lightly oiled double-thickness foil. Cook for 20–30 minutes either on the sides of the grid over hot coals or nestled in medium coals.

Serves 12.

Chocolate-stuffed Bananas with Crème de Cacao

6 firm bananas, unskinned
90 ml (6 tbsp) chocolate polka dots

20–30 ml (4–6 tsp) Crème de Cacao
15 ml (1 tbsp) sugar

Partially split, through the curved side, the full length of
each banana. Fill the slit with chocolate drops, Crème de
Cacao and sugar, then reshape the banana and wrap
tightly in foil. Nestle the packets in medium coals, or
round the sides of hot coals, and cook for about 10
minutes, turning the packets over once during the cooking
if this is possible.

Serves 6, but the recipe can be increased.

Honey Bananas

6 firm bananas
1 tbsp lemon juice
2 tbsp honey
2 tbsp butter

Peel the bananas and place each on a separate piece of
lightly oiled foil. Sprinkle with the lemon juice, then add
honey and butter without making any effort to spread
them.

Fold, wrap and cook the bananas over medium heat, or
around the sides of the grid, for 15 minutes, turning the
packets half-way through cooking. (The bananas will cook
more quickly in a covered barbecue.) Honey bananas
should be eaten as soon as they are cooked or they may
become too soft.

Serves 6, but the recipe may be increased.

Rolled Escalopes of Veal with Almonds and Cinzano Bianco

8 veal escalopes, beaten flat
Salt

Paprika
100 g (4 oz) butter
100 g (4 oz) flaked almonds
8 tbsp Cinzano Bianco

Put each piece of veal on a separate large square of lightly oiled double-thickness foil. Sprinkle with salt and paprika, then top each with 15 g (½ oz) of the butter and 15 g (½ oz) of the almonds. Sprinkle a tablespoon of Cinzano over each escalope and roll up Swiss-roll fashion.

Flat wrap the veal rolls in the foil and cook on the grid over medium coals for 45–60 minutes, turning the packets over half-way through. Serve the packets unopened on individual plates.

Serves 8.

Easy Baked Aubergine with Fondue Sauce

6 medium aubergines
175 g (6 oz) butter
15 ml (1 level tbsp) salt

Fondue sauce
350 g (12 oz) grated Gruyère cheese
2 level tsp cornflour
300 ml (½ pt) dry white wine

Wash and dry the aubergines and prick thoroughly all over. Melt the butter and stir in the salt, then brush generously over the aubergines. Wrap the aubergines loosely in the foil and twist the ends in Christmas-cracker fashion. Nestle the foil bundles in hot or medium coals around the sides of the barbecue and cook for about 30 minutes.

Meanwhile make the fondue sauce. Mix the cheese and cornflour thoroughly together in a foil dish, then pour in the wine. Place on the grid and heat until the mixture bubbles and thickens slightly. Set aside to keep warm.

On a side table cut through the aubergine packets lengthwise and spread the contents with the fondue sauce.

Serves 6–12, but the recipe can be increased.

Texan Hotsup Drumsticks

12 chicken legs

For the sauce
60 ml (4 tbsp) tomato purée
45 ml (3 tbsp) malt vinegar
30 ml (2 tbsp) fresh lemon juice
30 ml (2 tbsp) Worcestershire sauce
40 g (1½ oz) soft dark brown sugar
10 ml (2 tsp) salt
2½ ml (½ tsp) freshly ground black pepper
5 ml (1 tsp) mustard powder
5 ml (1 tsp) chilli powder
5 ml (1 tsp) paprika
30 ml (2 tbsp) vegetable oil
4 canned pimientoes, finely chopped

Make the sauce by mixing all the ingredients together in a saucepan, adding 2 tbsp of water if the sauce is too thick. Add the chicken legs and turn so that they are completely coated. Cook and leave to stand for 2 hours.

Fold wrap the chicken legs singly or two at a time in oiled foil, spooning the sauce generously over the chicken. Cover on the grid over medium heat for 30–40 minutes, turning the packets over at least once during cooking.

Serves 6–12, but the recipe may be increased.

Triple Lamb Chops en Papillote

For each portion you will need one piece of best-end neck of lamb with three bones. Ask the butcher to cut this for you.

6 lamb chops of triple thickness
Salt
Pepper
2 tbsp lemon juice
1 level tbsp dried oregano
1 level tbsp dried thyme
1–2 tbsp vegetable oil

Place each piece of lamb on a large sheet of triple-thickness foil. Sprinkle generously with salt, pepper, lemon juice, herbs and oil. Turn the chops over so that they are coated on both sides with the oil and herbs and then flat wrap them to seal.

Place the packets on the grid over medium coals and cover with the barbecue's lid or make a foil dome. Cook for about 30 minutes, turning each papillote over half-way through cooking. At the same time push the parcels towards the cooler outside part of the grid.

Serves 6, but the recipe can be increased.

Hungarian Lamb Chops

6 lean lamb chump chops, average thickness
½ green pepper, finely sliced
½ red pepper, finely sliced
1 medium onion, peeled and finely sliced
200 ml (7 fl oz) red wine
7 tbsp vegetable oil
6 level tbsp tomato purée
1 level tbsp (the hot variety) paprika
Salt
Pepper

Remove every vestige of fat from the chops, and place them in a large bowl with all the other ingredients. Stir thoroughly and leave to marinade for at least 12 hours, stirring occasionally.

Cut six 30 cm (12 in) squares of foil and place a lamb chop in the centre of each. Cover with the vegetables, scooping them from the marinade with a slotted spoon. (There should be about 1 tbsp marinade liquid on each chop.)

Flat wrap the chops securely and place on an uncovered grid, sealed side uppermost (the chops are not turned over during cooking). Cook for 15 minutes over medium coals or on the sides of a hot grid.

Serves 6, but the recipe can be increased.

Foil-baked Corn on the Cob

1 fresh corn cob per person
Butter

Remove the silk from the corn (there is no need to remove the husks). Place each corn cob on a piece of oiled foil, add a generous knob of butter and 2–3 tsp water. Wrap up tightly and nestle the packets in medium coals, to cook for 15–20 minutes, turning the packets half-way through.

If it is more convenient, cook the corn packets on the grid but allow about 20–30 minutes' cooking time. If corn is overcooked, it becomes brown and caramelized and the kernels dry up, so do inspect after the recommended time has elapsed.

Frozen corn on the cob can be treated in a similar way.

Take care when opening the foil packets as the corn is very hot indeed; it will retain its heat for some 15–20 minutes after cooking provided it is not unwrapped.

Whole Tomatoes in Foil

Simply wash firm tomatoes and wrap each tightly in foil. Cook on the sides of the grid over medium coals for about 10 minutes, turning the packets over once during cooking.

The tomatoes *can* be wrapped together in one packet but they may become squashed as you try to remove them from the foil.

Foil-baked Stuffed Edam Cheese

    1 Edam cheese, weight about 2 kg (4½ lb)
    175 g (6 oz) cooked shelled prawns
    1 small onion, finely chopped
    25 g (1 oz) butter
    2 tomatoes, skinned and chopped
    Salt
    Pepper
    25 g (1 oz) fresh breadcrumbs
    2 stoned green olives, sliced
    4 capers, chopped
    1 egg, beaten

Peel away the red covering from the cheese. Remove a 2½ cm (1 in) thick slice from the top of the cheese and set aside. Leaving a wall about 1 cm (½ in) thick, scoop the cheese out of the larger section. Keep about half the cheese for use in other dishes and chop the remainder finely. Put this into a mixing bowl with the prawns.

In a medium saucepan sauté the onion in the butter, then stir in the tomatoes and season with salt and pepper. Cook over gentle heat until all the liquid has evaporated.

Combine the cheese and tomato mixtures in the bowl, then add the breadcrumbs, olives, capers and bind with beaten egg. Fill the cheese cavity with the mixture and then replace the reserved cheese lid.

Wrap the whole cheese tightly in triple-thickness foil and nestle into medium coals. Cook for about 25–35

minutes or until you can feel some 'give' when you press
the foil package. Remove the package from the coals,
slice off the top through the foil. Scoop out the filling and
serve with crusty French bread.

Serves 12.

Barbecued Garlic Bread

1 French loaf
175 g (6 oz) garlic butter (see page 155)

Cut the loaf into 1.8 cm (¾ in) to 2.5 cm (1 in) slices but
do not sever at the bottom. Spread the garlic butter
thickly between each slice and wrap the loaf in foil. Cook
on the grid over medium coals for 15–20 minutes, turning
the parcel over frequently. Make sure that the foil is
folded tightly around the bread during cooking.

Not everybody likes garlic bread, so substitute another
flavoured butter if you prefer.

Jacket Potatoes

Choose medium-sized evenly shaped potatoes, scrub and
dry. Prick the skins thoroughly and deeply and rub with
oil or saffron butter. Wrap the potatoes in a double
thickness of foil and bake in the coals for about 45
minutes, turning the potatoes over occasionally.

It is not always easy to cook the potatoes in foil in the
coals because of the difficulty of getting them out when
there may be other food cooking on the grid. Alternative
methods are to bake the potatoes unwrapped in a conventional oven at 200°C(400°F) Gas 6 for about 1 hour, then
wrap and transfer them to the sides of the barbecue. Or
partly bake in the conventional oven, then wrap in foil and
finish cooking towards the centre of the grid over medium

coals. You can also par-boil the potatoes before baking but it is not a method that I really like.

When the potatoes feel soft to the touch, cut a deep cross through the foil and pull the sides open so that the gaps are made larger and fill with any of the savoury butters (see page 149) or unflavoured butter, season with salt and pepper and top with soured cream and freshly chopped chives.

Jacket potatoes do not have to be wrapped for success-ful cooking but they will have blackened crisp skins – which some people prefer.

8

Frying

Nutburgers
Middle Eastern Kofta
Beef and Sausage Burgers
Andalusian Steak with Tomatoes Xeres
Keftedhes Aya Naba
Hopi Chile Rolls
Peaches with Grand Marnier Flambé
Lemon-marinaded Sausages
Frizzled Vegetables
Ham and Cheese Roll-ups with Green Mayonnaise
Battered Sliced Aubergines
Crêpes Suzette

Nutburgers

225 g (8 oz) shelled hazelnuts, grated
225 g (8 oz) fresh breadcrumbs
225 g (8 oz) frozen peas, part thawed and chopped
2 eggs, beaten
15 ml (1 tbsp) Marmite

Mix all the ingredients thoroughly together, then divide
into eight 5 cm (2 in) × 1 cm (½ in) patties. Brush with
oil and grill over medium heat or fry in a lightly oiled pan
over high heat for about 10 minutes, turning the burgers
over once during cooking. This recipe can be made
entirely in the food processor using shelled whole nuts and
sliced bread, chopped together with peas. Serves 4 to 8,
but the recipe can be increased.

Middle Eastern Kofta

900 g (2 lb) lamb, cubed
2 large onions
25 g (1 oz) parsley sprigs, stalks removed
10 ml (2 tsp) salt
2.5 ml (½ tsp) mixed ground spice
2.5 ml (½ tsp) grated nutmeg
1.25 ml (¼ tsp) paprika
Vegetable oil for cooking

Mince the lamb, onions and parsley together, then mix
thoroughly with the salt, spice, nutmeg and paprika.
Shape into twelve ovals, then flatten gently with the palm
of the hand. Brush with oil and cook for about 8–10
minutes in a frying pan or on the grid lined with single-
thickness foil.

Serve with a salad of finely shredded lettuce and spring onions and pitta bread.

Serves 6, but the recipe can be increased.

Beef and Sausage Burgers

> 1 large onion, peeled and finely chopped
> 25 g (1 oz) butter
> 40 g (1½ oz) fresh breadcrumbs
> 900 g (2 lb) raw minced beef
> 2 eggs, beaten
> Salt and pepper
> 100 g (4 oz) pork sausage meat
> 1 level tbsp dried parsley

Lightly fry the onion in the butter. Drain and mix with the breadcrumbs, beef and eggs; season to taste. In a separate bowl, mix together the sausage meat and the parsley. Divide the beef mixture into sixteen portions and shape into 1 cm (¼ in) thick burgers. Divide the sausage meat into eight similar shapes, making them the same diameter as the beefburgers. Sandwich two beefburgers with one of sausage meat and press well down, reshaping if necessary.

Fry the burgers in a heavy-based pan on the grid over hot coals, turning over once during cooking. (You can grill the burgers if you like but there will be more spattering, as sausage meat tends to be fatty.) Allow 6–8 minutes' cooking on each side.

Serves 8, but the recipe may be increased.

Andalusian Steak with Tomatoes Xeres

> 1 large onion, skinned and finely chopped
> Olive oil
> 900 g (2 lb) raw minced beef

Salt
Pepper
1 egg, beaten
100 g (4 oz) dried breadcrumbs

For the sauce
  6 tomatoes, skinned, seeded and chopped
  2 cloves garlic, skinned and finely chopped
  1 heaped tbsp freshly chopped parsley
  Olive oil
  2 tbsp dry sherry
  Salt
  Pepper

First make the sauce. Place the tomatoes, half the garlic and the parsley into a small saucepan and stir in 1 tbsp of olive oil. Cook over gentle heat until the tomatoes are soft. Stir in the sherry and season the mixture with salt and pepper. Cover and set aside.

To make the steaks, first sauté the onion and the remaining garlic in 1 tbsp of oil. Remove from the heat, mix in the meat and add salt and pepper to taste.

Divide the meat into six portions and shape into oval patties about 1 cm (½ in) thick. Dip individually in the beaten egg and coat in breadcrumbs. Refrigerate for half an hour or until required.

Fry the patties on the barbecue for 8 to 10 minutes in a heavy-based frying pan in 1 or 2 tbsp of olive oil, turning the patties over half-way through cooking.

Reheat the sauce in the kitchen and keep hot on the barbecue grid. To serve, spoon a little sauce over each steak.

Serves 6, but the recipe can be increased.

Keftedhes Aya Naba

900 g (2 lb) trimmed leg of lamb, minced
1 small onion, skinned and very finely chopped
½ tsp grated nutmeg
Salt
Pepper
75 g (3 oz) pine nuts, chopped
Vegetable oil

Mix the lamb, onion and nutmeg together and season with salt and pepper to taste. Stir in the pine nuts and bind well together.

Divide the mixture into twelve balls and flatten to a depth of 1 cm (½ in). Brush the patties with oil and cook in an ungreased frying pan or metal sheet over medium coals for about 8–10 minutes, turning them over half-way through cooking.

Serves 4–6, but the recipe may be increased.

Note: These patties are nice served without a sauce but accompanied by a green salad sprinkled with cheese.

Hopi Chile Rolls

450 g (1 lb) cooked lamb or beef, finely minced
1 medium onion, finely chopped
1 level tsp salt
1 level tbsp chilli compound powder

For the dough
450 g (1 lb) plain flour
2.5 ml (½ tsp) salt
1 level tbsp baking powder
50 g (2 oz) white cooking fat
3 level tbsp dried skimmed milk
5 tbsp milk

Mix the meat, onion, salt and chilli powder together in a bowl and set aside.

To make the dough, sift the flour, salt and baking powder together, then rub in the cooking fat. Stir in the dried milk powder and mix to a soft dough with the milk.

Divide the dough into twelve pieces and flatten each one into a circle about 12.5 cm (5 in) in diameter. Spoon some of the meat into the centre of each circle, then brush the edges with water and draw them up over the meat filling, dolly-bag fashion, pressing the dough at the top so that it is well sealed. Turn the rolls over and flatten slightly.

Bake on a flat well-oiled sheet of double-thickness foil over hot coals in a covered grill for about 20 minutes. Serve with a green side salad and hot or cold Spanish sauce (see page 143).

Makes 12

Peaches with Grand Marnier Flambé

    75 g (3 oz) butter
    65 g (2½ oz) caster sugar
    4 tsp lemon juice
    6 large ripe peaches, skinned
    1 tbsp Grand Marnier

Put the butter in a heavy frying pan on the barbecue grid over hot coals. When the butter has melted, stir in the sugar and the lemon juice, then add the peaches, turning them over and stirring them round for about 5 minutes until the sugar caramelizes. Add the Grand Marnier, ignite with a taper, and serve hot.

Serves 6, but the recipe can be increased if you have a larger frying pan.

Lemon-marinaded Sausages

    8 large sausages
    7 tbsp vegetable oil
    2 level tbsp French mustard
    Juice of ½ lemon
    Salt
    Pepper
    25 g (1 oz) butter

Prick the sausages thoroughly all over – this is important, to enable them to absorb the marinade. In a shallow dish, combine the oil, mustard and lemon juice, with salt and pepper to taste. Place the sausages in the marinade then cover and refrigerate for 6–8 hours, turning the sausages occasionally.

To cook, remove the sausages from the marinade and fry them in the butter in a large heavy-based frying pan on the barbecue grid over hot coals for about 15 minutes, turning the sausages frequently.

Serves 6–8, which is the maximum number of sausages it is possible to get in a large frying pan. Increase the marinade and the number of sausages if you like, but you will have to fry in batches.

Frizzled Vegetables

    50 g (2 oz) butter
    Garlic powder
    ¼ tsp celery salt
    Pepper
    6 large field mushrooms, wiped and peeled
    1 large Spanish onion, skinned and sliced into rings
    6 large tomatoes, peeled and halved
    1 heaped tbsp fresh breadcrumbs

Put a large shallow foil dish on the grid over hot coals and add the butter, sprinkling with the garlic powder, celery salt and pepper. Spread out the mushrooms, onion slices and tomatoes in the dish and cook for about 10 minutes, removing the tomatoes as soon as they are ready.

When the mushrooms and onions are tender, transfer to a serving platter, piling the onions and tomatoes on top of the mushrooms. Spoon the residual juices over the vegetables, then sprinkle the breadcrumbs into the dish and stir until they are brown and have absorbed the remaining butter. Sprinkle the crumbs on top of the vegetables.

Serves 6. It is difficult to increase this recipe as there is only limited space on a large foil dish.

Ham and Cheese Roll-ups with Green Mayonnaise

6 square slices cooked ham
175 g (6 oz) Cheddar cheese in an even-shaped block
150 ml (¼ pt) green mayonnaise (see page 160)

Cut the cheese into 6 thick sticks the width of the ham. Place a cheese stick on one edge of each slice of ham and roll up.

Cook the ham rolls seam-side down on a treble-thickness-foil sheet on the grid over hot coals, for about 5 minutes, or until the cheese begins to melt. Turn the ham rolls over half-way through cooking.

Serve on plates with green mayonnaise.

Serves 6, but the recipe can be increased.

Battered Sliced Aubergines

3 medium aubergines
75 to 100 g (3 to 4 oz) chickpea or gram flour
½ tsp ground cardamom
Salt
Pepper
Vegetable oil

Slice the aubergines into 1 cm (½ in) thick slices. Place them in a pan of boiling salted water and cook for 3–4 minutes. Drain and cool.

Mix the chickpea or gram flour with the ground cardamom and season with a little salt and pepper. Add sufficient cold water to form a smooth thick paste. Fold in the aubergine slices and turn well to coat.

Pour a few tablespoons of vegetable oil into a large heavy-based frying pan. Heat over hot coals on the barbecue grid and when the oil sizzles shallow-fry the aubergine slices. Serve hot as a vegetarian main course with rice, or as a vegetable.

Serves 4–6. The recipe can be increased provided you are prepared to fry in batches.

Crêpes Suzette

    18 small thin pancakes
    100 g (4 oz) granulated sugar
    2 oranges
    2 lemons
    4 tbsp brandy
    4 tbsp Curaçao
    100 g (4 oz) unsalted butter

To flambé
    2–3 tbsp sugar
    3 tbsp brandy

Stack the freshly cooked pancakes between sheets of greaseproof paper, cover and set aside.

Put the sugar into a large jug or lipped bowl and holding the oranges and lemons over the jug or bowl, score the skins with the prongs of a fork so that the zest drops on to the sugar.

Halve the oranges and lemons, squeeze out the juice

and add it to the jug with the brandy and Curaçao. Stir thoroughly until dissolved. Cover and set aside until required.

Put the unsalted butter into a small dish, the sugar for flambé into a sugar shaker and keep the brandy to be used for flambéing in the bottle. Store these, the sauce and the pancakes within reach of the barbecue.

On the grid over hot coals, using a heavy-based frying pan, melt a little of the butter and add 1–2 tbsp of the sauce and stir to form a creamy mixture. Slide in one pancake, fold it into four and push it to the side of the pan; add a little more butter and a little more sauce and another pancake, fold into four and push to the side of the pan; repeat this process until the pan is full of folded soaked pancakes.

Shake a little sugar from the shaker over the pancakes, pour over a spoonful of brandy, then ignite with a taper. Serve as soon as the flames have subsided.

You will probably only be able to get about half the pancakes into the pan at one time. You can therefore either prepare the Crêpes Suzette in two batches or have two frying pans on the barbecue.

Serves 6, but the recipe can be increased.

9

On Skewers

Gammon and Green Pepper Kebabs with Tomato and
   Honey Sauce
Brandied Five-fruit Kebabs
Aloo Kebabs
Taos Kebabs
Brochettes de Boeuf
Seafood Brochettes
Kidney Kebabs
Chip Kebabs
Skewered Chicken and Green Peppers
Chicken and Grapefruit Kebabs
Malaysian Satay in Peanut Sauce
Skewered Vegetables

Gammon and Green Pepper Kebabs with Tomato and Honey Sauce

  6 gammon steaks, 1–1.5 cm (½–¾ in) thick, cut into
    bite-sized chunks
  2 large green peppers, seeded and cut into 4 cm (1½ in)
    pieces

For the sauce
  1 × 227 g (8 oz) can tomatoes
  1 small onion, peeled and quartered
  45 ml (3 tbsp) wine vinegar
  90 ml (6 tbsp) clear honey
  5 ml (1 level tsp) paprika
  15 ml (1 tbsp) tomato purée
  Salt and pepper

To make the sauce, blend all the ingredients together in
the liquidizer until smooth.

Stir the gammon and green peppers into the same
mixture and marinate for 2 hours. After marinading
thread the gammon and peppers on to skewers.

Pour the sauce marinade into a heavy-based unlidded
saucepan. Bring to the boil on the grid, then move the pan
to where the heat is less and cook for 5–10 minutes or until
the sauce is thick. Pour the sauce into a smaller saucepan
or foil basin and set on the side of the grid to keep warm.

Cook the skewered gammon and peppers over medium
coals for about 10 minutes. Serve the kebabs accompanied
by the sauce.

Serves 6, but the quantities can be increased.

Brandied Five-fruit Kebabs

½ medium pineapple, peeled
2 satsumas, peeled
2 firm peaches, unskinned
2 bananas
2 dessert apples
75 g (3 oz) butter
40 g (1½ oz) icing sugar
45 ml (3 tbsp) brandy

Prepare the fruit in the following order:
(1) Cut the pineapple into 2½ cm (1 in) chunks.
(2) Divide each satsuma into about four sections.
(3) Halve and stone the peaches and cut each half into four.
(4) Peel and cut each banana into 2.5 cm (1 in) slices.
(5) Quarter and core the apples and then cut each quarter in half.

Thread the fruit alternately on to long skewers, leaving 2.5 cm (1 in) space at each end, starting and finishing with either pineapple or apple.

Melt the butter in a small saucepan and stir in the icing sugar. Remove from the heat and add the brandy.

Brush the mixture lightly over the kebabs, then grill over medium heat for about 6–7 minutes, basting occasionally with the sauce. Brush with the remaining sauce just before serving.

Serves 6–8, but the recipe can be increased.

Aloo Kebabs

900 g (2 lb) potatoes
60–90 ml (4–6 tbsp) bottled curry paste

Peel the potatoes and cut into 4–5 cm (1½–2 in) chunks.

Boil in salted water until a skewer can be pushed through with slight pressure. Drain thoroughly.

While still warm, thread the potatoes on to skewers and brush with the curry paste. Leave for 30 minutes, then grill over hot coals for 10–12 minutes, turning the skewers from time to time until the potatoes are dry and flaky on the outside.

Serves 6, but the recipe can be increased.

Taos Kebabs

450 g (1 lb) lean pork, trimmed and cubed
450 g (1 lb) rump steak, trimmed and cubed
3 fresh chillis
2 cloves garlic, peeled and crushed
1 level tsp ground cumin
3 tbsp vegetable oil
2 tbsp lemon juice
1 × 397 g (14 oz) can tomatoes
Salt
Pepper

Grill the chillis under fierce heat on the conventional cooker until the skin blisters. Do not touch the chillis with your hands – rather use a pair of tongs. (The chillis can also be blistered on the barbecue in the hot coals.)

Wearing rubber gloves and using a knife and fork, remove the peel. Cut the chillis in half lengthwise and scrape out the seeds. Chop the flesh then blend with the garlic, cumin, oil, lemon juice, tomatoes and their juice in the liquidizer, seasoning with salt and pepper.

Pour the mixture into a bowl and stir in the cubed meat. Stand the bowl in a cool place for several hours and stir from time to time so that all the meat is well coated.

Thread the pork and beef cubes alternately on to skewers, leaving a small space between each piece, and cook on the grid over medium coals for 20 minutes, turning the skewers and frequently basting with the marinade.

Serves 6, but the marinade is sufficient for an extra 450 g (1 lb) of meat.

Brochettes de Boeuf

900 g (2 lb) trimmed frying steak, cut into 4 cm (1½ in) cubes
150 ml (¼ pt) good quality vegetable oil
¾ tsp freshly ground black pepper
1 large red pepper, skinned
1 large yellow pepper, skinned
175 g (6 oz) smoked streaky bacon, de-rinded and cut into 2½ cm (1 in) slices
12 button mushrooms, wiped
6 tomatoes, skinned and halved crosswise
6 baby onions, skinned and halved crosswise
16–18 sage leaves
Salt
350 g (12 oz) long-grain rice, freshly cooked or reheated

Toss the meat in the oil in a large bowl and mix in the freshly ground black pepper. Leave to stand for at least 30 minutes.

While the meat is marinading, skin the peppers. To do this, either hold with a fork over a gas flame or grill on the barbecue grid until the skins shrivel. Cut the skinned peppers in half lengthwise, remove the cores and seeds and then slice into 1 cm (½ in) strips crosswise.

When all the vegetables have been prepared and the coals are ready, start to thread the skewers. Begin with the mushrooms, then add the beef, peppers, bacon, tomatoes and onions, separating each with a sage leaf.

Cook over medium coals for about 20 minutes, basting with the oil marinade and turning the skewers frequently. Season with salt towards the end of the cooking time.

Serve on or accompanied by the hot rice.

Serves 6, but the recipe can be increased.

Seafood Brochettes

700 g (1½ lb) scallops off the shell
700 g (1½ lb) scampi tails
450 ml (¾ pt) white wine
3 tbsp vegetable oil
2 level tbsp chopped fresh chervil, or 1 level tsp dried chervil
1 level tbsp freshly ground black pepper
Salt
Melted butter for basting

For serving
Béarnaise sauce (see page 138)
Lemon wedges

Trim away the stringy membranes and cut the scallops in half if they are the big variety. Put them into a mixing bowl with the scampi tails. Add the wine, oil, chervil, pepper and salt to taste and stir once. Cover and refrigerate for several hours, gently stirring occasionally.

Thread the scallops and scampi tails on to skewers and brush with melted butter. Cook over hot coals for about 5–6 minutes, turning the skewers and brushing with butter frequently during cooking.

Serve with Béarnaise sauce (page 138) and lemon wedges.

Serves 6, but the recipe can be increased.

Kidney Kebabs

> 12 lambs' kidneys, skinned and cored
> Salt
> Pepper
> Melted butter

For serving
> Mustard butter (see page 151)

Cut through the kidneys horizontally from the core side
(but do not completely sever the two halves). Open out
the kidneys so that they resemble a butterfly shape.
Thread the skewers through the kidneys in a zig-zag
motion. Season with salt and pepper and brush with the
melted butter.

Cook over hot coals for 4–5 minutes, turning the
skewers frequently and basting each time with the butter.
Do not overcook; the kidneys should still be slightly pink
inside. Serve pats of mustard butter separately.

Serves 6.

Chip Kebabs

> 1 lb frozen chunky chips

Separate the chips and leave until partly thawed. Thread
on to skewers and cook over hot coals for about 10
minutes, turning the kebabs once during cooking.

It is better to thread the chips when partly thawed, as
they become very soft and unmanageable when fully
thawed.

Serves 4, but the recipe can be increased.

Skewered Chicken and Green Peppers

6 boned chicken breasts, skins removed
4 tbsp soy sauce
1 rounded tbsp demerara sugar
1 level tsp salt
⅛ level tsp ground black pepper
1.25 ml (¼ tsp) garlic powder
1.25 ml (¼ tsp) ground ginger
2 green peppers, cored, seeded and cut into 1 cm (½ in) dice
100 g (4 oz) button mushrooms
45 ml (3 tbsp) clear honey

Cut the chicken into 2.5 cm (1 in) pieces. Mix together in a large bowl the soy sauce, sugar, salt, pepper, garlic powder and ginger. Add the chicken pieces, toss thoroughly and set aside for 2 hours.

Bring a small pan of water to the boil, then add the green peppers and mushrooms. Bring back to the boil and cook for 2 minutes. Drain.

Thread the chicken, peppers and mushrooms on to skewers and brush with the marinade. Cook on the grid over medium coals for about 20 minutes, turning the skewers frequently and brushing occasionally with the marinade. Towards the end of the cooking time brush with the honey.

Serves 4–6, but the recipe can be increased.

Chicken and Grapefruit Kebabs

1 × 1.6 kg (3½ lb) oven-ready chicken
6 tbsp olive oil
3 grapefruit
Salt
Pepper

225 g (½ lb) gammon
Paprika

Skin and bone the chicken and cut the flesh into 2 cm (1½ in) chunks. Put into a large bowl with the oil and the juice of one half-grapefruit. Season with salt and pepper and mix thoroughly.

Trim the gammon and cut into strips 2 cm (1½ in) long and about 1 cm (½ in) thick and add to the marinade. Cover and leave to marinate for at least 6 hours.

Peel and segment the remaining grapefruit, removing as much of the white pith as possible.

When ready, thread the chicken and gammon strips on to skewers alternately with the grapefruit segments and sprinkle with the paprika. Cook over medium coals for about 15 minutes, turning the skewers and brushing with marinade a few times during cooking.

Serves 6, but the recipe can be increased.

Malaysian Satay in Peanut Sauce

225 g (½ lb) raw prawns, peeled and de-veined
225 g (½ lb) raw chicken, cubed
225 g (½ lb) pork fillet, cubed
225 g (½ lb) rump steak, cubed
1 large cucumber
Salt
350 g (12 oz) freshly cooked rice

For the sauce
150 g (5 oz) roasted peanuts, finely ground
2 level tsp ground coriander
1 level tsp ground cumin
¼ tsp chilli powder
½ tsp ground ginger
1 small onion, finely chopped

2 level tsp shrimp paste
1 level tsp salt
25 g (1 oz) desiccated coconut
150 ml (¼ pt) evaporated milk
150 ml (¼ pt) water
Juice of 1 lemon
Pinch sugar
2 tbsp vegetable oil

Make the sauce by mixing together all the ingredients in a large saucepan.

Stir in the prawns, chicken and meats, cover and leave to marinate for 2 hours.

Meanwhile peel the cucumber, halve it lengthways, then halve each section lengthways again. Cut into 1 cm (½ in) slices. Place in a bowl and sprinkle with salt.

After marinating, remove the meats, prawns and chicken from the saucepan and thread on skewers.

Bring the marinade to the boil on the hob, then lower the heat and simmer for 5 minutes or until thick. Pour the marinade into a double-thickness-foil basin or small saucepan and place on the side of the barbecue to keep hot.

Drain the cucumber and put into a serving dish.

Cook the skewered meats and seafood on the grid over hot coals for about 10 minutes, basting occasionally with the sauce and turning the skewers frequently. Do not overcook or the prawns will become dried up inside.

Serve with a few spoonsful of the hot sauce and plain boiled rice and offer the cucumber separately.

Serves 6, but the recipe can be increased.

Skewered Vegetables

Not all vegetables will cook at the same time, so that if you wish to thread a mixture of vegetables on to skewers, you will have to par-cook some of them first. Mushrooms, green and red peppers, courgettes and tomatoes need no prior attention but carrots, onions, aubergines and potatoes should be par-boiled for about 3 minutes. The thinner the slice or the smaller the chunk, the quicker the cooking will be. It is attractive to thread skewers with just one or two varieties and this is sometimes more acceptable to guests who may not like all types. Try three or four different coloured peppers including black, yellow, green and red. Courgettes and par-cooked aubergines cook happily together as do onions and potatoes. Brush the vegetables with plain or any flavoured butter and cook on the grid over medium coals.

Skewered tomatoes will take only about 5 minutes while carrots could take up to 30 minutes. Mushrooms will take about 5 minutes and potatoes 30–35 minutes.

10

Barbecue Sauces, Marinades and Sundries

Apple Barbecue Sauce
All-purpose Barbecue Sauce
Quickly Made Barbecue Sauce
Chilli Sauce
Teryaki Marinade for Fish
Tortillas
Nan
Garlic Sauce
Hollandaise Sauce
Easy Béarnaise Sauce
Hot Barbecue Sauce
Curried Seafood Cocktail

Apple Barbecue Sauce

1 medium onion, skinned and finely chopped
1 small green pepper, cored, seeded and finely chopped
1 clove garlic, skinned and crushed
½ dessert apple, peeled, cored and finely chopped
300 ml (½ pt) chicken stock
30 ml (2 level tbsp) redcurrant jelly
1 level tbsp tomato purée
1 tsp Worcestershire sauce
1 tsp fresh lemon juice
1 tsp arrowroot blended with 1 tbsp cold water

Put all the ingredients into a heavy-based saucepan and bring to the boil over gentle heat, stirring continuously. Reduce the heat and, still stirring, simmer for 5 minutes or until the sauce thickens. Store in a jar, covered with a jam-pot cover and screw-top lid. Makes about 300 ml (½pt).

All-purpose Barbecue Sauce

1 tbsp vegetable oil
1 medium onion, skinned and finely chopped
2 celery stalks, finely sliced
3 tbsp red wine vinegar
3 level tbsp tomato ketchup
1 tbsp Worcestershire sauce
Juice of ½ lemon
300 ml (½ pt) well-flavoured chicken stock
1 × 396 g (14 oz) can tomatoes
Bouquet garni

Salt
Pepper

Put the oil in a heavy-based saucepan and stir in the onion
and celery. Cook over gentle heat until the onion and
celery are soft. Add all the remaining ingredients, seasoning to taste with salt and pepper. Bring to the boil, then
reduce the heat and simmer for 30 minutes, stirring
occasionally. Remove the bouquet garni. Store as Apple
Barbecue Sauce. Makes about 300 ml (½ pt).

Quickly Made Barbecue Sauce

450 ml (¾ pt) bottled tomato ketchup
Shake Tabasco sauce
3 tbsp malt vinegar
1 level tsp paprika
½ level tsp garlic powder

Mix all the ingredients together thoroughly, then cover
and use as required. Store as Apple Barbecue Sauce.
Makes about 450 ml (¾ pt).

Chilli Sauce

50 g (2 oz) butter
1 medium onion, finely chopped
1 clove garlic, crushed
2.5 ml (½ tsp) ground ginger
25 ml (1½ level tbsp) chilli powder
300 ml (½ pt) tomato purée
150 ml (¼ pt) malt vinegar
25 g (1 oz) demerara sugar
15 ml (1 tbsp) Worcestershire sauce
10 ml (2 tsp) salt

Melt the butter in a pan and fry the onion and garlic until
golden brown. Add the remaining ingredients and stir in

150 ml (¼ pt) water. Bring to the boil and simmer for 10 minutes, stirring constantly, or until the sauce is thick. Store as Apple Barbecue Sauce. Makes about 450 ml (¾ pt).

Teryaki Marinade for Fish

90 ml (6 tbsp) dark soy sauce
90 ml (6 tbsp) sweet white wine
90 ml (6 tbsp) medium or dry sherry
1 clove garlic, crushed

Put all the ingredients into a saucepan and bring to the boil. Pour over the raw fish and leave for 30 minutes. Brush the fish with the marinade during the cooking process. Makes about 300 ml (½pt).

Tortillas

225 g (8 oz) plain flour
1 level tsp salt
50 g (2 oz) white cooking fat
6–7 tbsp warm water

Sift the flour and salt into a mixing bowl and mix in the fat with a fork. Add the water gradually and knead to a soft but manageable dough. Wrap the dough in a greased polythene bag and refrigerate for 6–8 hours.

Divide the mixture into twelve portions, then shape into balls and roll out on a floured surface to thin pancake-shaped rounds. Use an upturned plate to trim to an even shape.

Heat an ungreased frying pan and cook each tortilla for 20 seconds on either side, or until brown patches appear. Store between sheets of cling film and wrap in a dry tea cloth until required.

Flour tortillas, which are served with a Mexican-type

barbecue, can be briefly reheated on the grid on the side of the barbecue.

Makes 12, but the recipe can be increased.

Nan

You can make nan at home, but if you have a curry house nearby it is probably easier to purchase it from there and then reheat on the side of the barbecue grill. However, here is the recipe if you want to do it yourself.

250 g (10 oz) strong plain flour
1 level tsp bicarbonate of soda
1 level tsp salt
1 level tsp sugar
5 tbsp milk
4 tbsp plain yogurt
1 egg
Vegetable oil

Sift the dry ingredients into a mixing bowl. Mix the milk and yogurt together and heat in a saucepan until lukewarm. Remove from the heat and beat in the egg. Pour the liquid into the flour mixture, add 1 tablespoon vegetable oil and mix to a soft dough. Add a little water if necessary and knead for about 5 minutes or until the mixture is no longer sticky. Oil the hands and rub over the dough. Cover the dough with a wet cloth (or put into a polythene bag) and leave to stand overnight.

Divide the dough into twelve portions, shape into balls and roll out on a floured surface into 10 cm (4 in) rounds. Cover with a wet cloth until needed.

Oil a heavy frying pan and bring to moderate heat on the conventional hob. Cook the nan one at a time, damp-side uppermost, until puffed up and crisp underneath. Transfer to a grill pan and brown under fierce heat while cooking the next nan in the pan. (Alternatively, nan can be deep fried in hot oil.) Keep warm on the side of the barbecue grill.

Makes 12, but the recipe can be increased.

Garlic Sauce

    6 cloves garlic, peeled
    ½ level tsp salt
    2 egg yolks
    300 ml (½ pt) vegetable oil
    2 tsp lemon juice

Crush the garlic, sprinkle with the salt and mash, using the flat blade of a table knife on a flat surface. Put the garlic into a small mixing bowl and beat in the egg yolks. Slowly beat in the oil, drop by drop, until the mixture becomes slightly thick. Now beat in the remaining oil a little more quickly, adding the lemon juice as the sauce continues to thicken.

Transfer the cooled sauce to a suitable container, cover tightly and refrigerate. The sauce will keep for 1–2 days in the refrigerator. Serve with fish or seafood.

Makes about 300 ml (½ pt).

Hollandaise Sauce

Hollandaise sauce is easy to make in the microwave oven but if you are cooking it conventionally, you may have to face the problem of curdling. This is a less-likely-to-curdle recipe.

    225 g (8 oz) unsalted butter
    Salt
    Pepper
    2 tbsp fresh lemon juice
    3 egg yolks

Cut the butter into several pieces and put into a bowl over a pan of hot water. (The water must not be boiling nor touch the base of the bowl and the pan should not be on the heat.) Beat the butter with a whisk until it is creamy but not liquid. Season with salt and pepper and beat in the lemon juice a few drops at a time. Add the beaten egg yolks a little at a time, beating constantly until the sauce is well blended.

Put the saucepan over just a thread of heat and whisk the sauce thoroughly and briskly until the mixture thickens. Remove the pan from the heat, take the bowl from the pan and continue whisking as the sauce cools and thickens. Store in the refrigerator for 24 hours in a covered dish. The sauce can be frozen and reconstituted in the microwave oven. Makes about 300 ml (½ pt).

Easy Béarnaise Sauce

    3 egg yolks
    5 tbsp tarragon vinegar
    Pinch salt
    Pinch mustard powder
    Pepper
    100 g (4 oz) butter
    ½ level tsp dried tarragon
    ½ level tsp dried chervil
    4 tbsp dry white wine

Blend together the egg yolks, 3 tbsp tarragon vinegar, salt, mustard and pepper in the food processor or liquidizer goblet at high speed.

In a small saucepan heat the butter until it is liquid and bubbling but not brown. Switch on the processor at high speed and pour the butter into the egg mixture in a steady stream. When the mixture is thick pour it into a jug or mixing bowl.

Put the dried herbs, wine, and the remaining 2 tbsp

tarragon vinegar into the saucepan, bring to the boil, then simmer until reduced by half. Set aside to cool to the same temperature as the sauce mixture, then gently stir together. Store as Hollandaise Sauce. Makes about 300 ml (½ pt).

Hot Barbecue Sauce

1 medium onion, finely chopped
1 clove garlic, crushed
9 tbsp vegetable oil
1 level tsp salt
1 × 227 g (8 oz) can tomatoes
15–30 ml (1–2 level tbsp) chilli powder
4 tbsp malt vinegar

Fry the onion and garlic in a tablespoon of the oil until light brown. Stir in the remaining ingredients, bring to the boil, then simmer for about 5 minutes or until the sauce is thick. Store as Hollandaise Sauce. Makes just under 300 ml (½ pt).

Curried Seafood Cocktail

3 tbsp tomato ketchup
1 tsp Worcestershire sauce
Few drops Tabasco
150 ml (¼ pt) curried mayonnaise dip (page 145)
1 small lettuce heart
225 g (8 oz) shelled cooked prawns

For garnish
6 large whole prawns
Alfalfa

Stir the tomato ketchup, Worcestershire sauce and Tabasco into the curried mayonnaise. Shred the lettuce finely and divide between six tall glasses. (The lettuce should come about two-thirds the way up the glass.) Just before serving pile the shelled prawns on top of the lettuce, then top with the sauce and garnish with the alfalfa. Loop one whole prawn over the rim of each glass.

Serves 6, but the recipe can be increased.

11
Dips

Guacamole
Cold Spanish Sauce
Mustard Curd
Curried Mayonnaise Dip
Tequila Dip
Horseradish Dip
Raita
Instant Shrimp Dip
Louisiana Seafood Dip

Guacamole

1 small onion, peeled and quartered
1 clove garlic, peeled
2 tsp fresh lemon juice
2 large tomatoes, peeled and seeded
4 ripe avocados
Salt
Pepper

Blend the onion, garlic, 1 tsp lemon juice and the tomatoes in the liquidizer or food processor. Peel and stone the avocados, add to the mixture and process until well blended. Season with salt and pepper.

Pour the mixture into a bowl. Sprinkle with the remaining lemon juice, cover with cling film and refrigerate for 3–4 hours.

Serves 10, but the recipe can be increased.

Cold Spanish Sauce

This sauce can be served either with plainly grilled or roast meats or as a dip for left-over cold lamb chops or sausages.

1 medium onion, skinned and quartered
1 medium green pepper, cored, seeded and quartered
4 firm tomatoes, quartered
3 tbsp red wine vinegar
2 level tsp caster sugar
½ tsp celery salt

½ tsp dry mustard
Salt
Freshly ground black pepper

Place all the ingredients in the food processor, adding each item to the processor in the order in which it is given. Pour the resulting sauce into a serving dish and chill in the refrigerator for at least 12 hours.

Makes about 600 ml (1 pt).

Mustard Curd

Use as a dip for sausages, frankfurters and crisps, or serve as a sauce with pork or beef grills.

50 g (2 oz) dry mustard
¼ tsp freshly ground black pepper
Pinch white pepper
Pinch cayenne
¼ tsp salt
7 tbsp cider vinegar
100 g (4 oz) caster sugar
20 g (¾ oz) butter
1 egg, beaten

Blend the mustard, peppers and salt with the cider vinegar in a medium saucepan. Stir in the sugar. Slowly bring to the boil, stirring all the time. Remove from the heat, add the butter and stir until it is melted.

Blend the egg with 2 tbsp water, pour into the saucepan, then return to the heat and cook over gentle heat, stirring continuously until the sauce thickens. Adjust the seasoning, then pour the sauce into a jar or serving dish. Cover and refrigerate.

Makes about 300 ml (½ pt).

Curried Mayonnaise Dip

This dip is equally good when served as a sauce with fish or chicken dishes.

½ pt good quality mayonnaise
1 clove garlic, peeled and well crushed
1 tsp tarragon vinegar
¼ tsp ground ginger
¼ tsp ground cumin
¼ tsp ground coriander
¼ tsp turmeric
¼ tsp ground cardamom
Pinch chilli powder
Salt (if needed)

Mix all the ingredients thoroughly together, seasoning with salt if necessary. Pour the sauce into a serving dish, cover and chill in the refrigerator. (Do not store in the freezer.)

Makes about 300 ml (½ pt).

Tequila Dip

2 tbsp Tequila
45 ml (3 tbsp) demerara sugar
Finely grated rind of 1 lime
Finely grated rind of 1 orange
Finely grated rind of ½ lemon
1 tsp fresh lemon juice
Pinch ground ginger
Pinch ground cinnamon
25 g (1 oz) ground almonds
450 ml (¾ pt) soured cream

Mix all the ingredients together in a bowl then chill for 24 hours.
Stir thoroughly, then pour into the serving vessel. Serve

with a platter of sliced mango, pineapple, melon and fresh strawberries.

Makes 450 ml (¾ pt).

Horseradish Dip

    300 ml (½ pt) single cream
    1 tbsp fresh lemon juice
    150 ml (¼ pt) mayonnaise
    1.25 ml (¼ tsp) dry mustard
     2 level tbsp freshly grated horseradish

Mix the cream with the lemon juice and set aside for 1 hour until the cream begins to clot. Beat in all the remaining ingredients, then chill for 2–3 hours. Serve with frankfurters, cold sausages or beef kebabs.

Makes about 450 ml (¾ pt).

Raita

Basic sauce
    150 ml (¼ pt) thick set natural yogurt
    Salt
    Pepper

Variations
    (a) 1 × 5 cm (2 in) piece cucumber, peeled and cut into matchstick strips

    (b) 1 level tbsp finely chopped onion
        1 level tbsp finely chopped cucumber   } mixed
        1 small tomato, chopped   together
        1 tbsp freshly chopped coriander leaves
        1.25 ml (¼ tsp) ground ginger

(c) 1 level tsp finely chopped
     fresh mint
  1 level tsp grated zest of orange } mixed together

To make the basic sauce, beat the yogurt until smooth and season to taste with salt and pepper. To complete the sauce add any of the suggested variations, pour into an attractive serving bowl and chill for 1 hour.

Serve with a garnish that indicates the content of the Raita, i.e. thinly sliced cucumber, or onion rings, or orange slices.

Makes 150 ml (¼ pt).

Instant Shrimp Dip

Use this recipe as a dip for raw vegetables, or serve with grilled pork chops.

    1 × 198 g (7 oz) can shrimps, drained
    1 × 227 g (8 oz) carton cottage cheese
    3 level tbsp tomato ketchup
    ¼ small onion
    1 tsp lemon juice
    Dash Worcestershire sauce
    4 tbsp milk or single cream

Process all the ingredients in the blender or liquidizer until smooth. Pour into a serving dish and chill.

Makes about 300 ml (½ pt).

Louisiana Seafood Dip

Serve this hot dip as a starter with chunks of freshly cut French bread.

    2 × 298 g (10½ oz) cans condensed cream of mushroom
     soup

225 g (½ lb) button mushrooms, sliced
8 spring onions, peeled and thinly sliced
2 rounded tbsp freshly chopped parsley
1 level tsp paprika
1 level tsp freshly ground black pepper
450 g (1 lb) cooked peeled prawns
150 g (5 oz) canned dressed crab
150 ml (¼ pt) cream or natural yogurt

Put the soup, mushrooms, onions, parsley, paprika and pepper into a heavy-based saucepan and cook on the hob over gentle heat without boiling for 5 minutes. Stir in the prawns and crab meat and bring to just below boiling point.

Transfer the mixture to a metal casserole or deep foil dish and place on the side of the barbecue. Stir in the yogurt or cream.

Serves 6–8. The recipe can be increased but should be kept hot on the barbecue in the quantities given here.

12

Savoury Butters

Mustard Butter
Anchovy Butter
Egg and Onion Butter
Maître d'Hôtel Butter
Horseradish Butter
Walnut Butter
Caper Butter
Prawn Butter
Mushroom Butter
Garlic Butter
Orange Butter

Flavoured butters add a new dimension to plainly barbecued foods. They can be made well in advance and stored in the freezer or refrigerator. Serve them melted for easy spreading. (Melted butters are also easily added to the food during cooking.) Serve soft or hard in the form of a pat or a piped rosette for special-occasion barbecuing.

Since butter tends to burn, always add it towards the end of the cooking time when using as a spread during barbecuing.

Flavoured butter can also be used in foil cookery, brushing the food with the butter before cooking.

Of course, margarine may be substituted for butter if preferred.

Mustard Butter

For use with red meat, kidney or liver.

100 g (4 oz) unsalted butter
30 ml (2 tbsp) Moutarde de Meaux
Salt
Pepper

Beat the butter until soft and fluffy, then beat in the mustard and season to taste with salt and pepper.

Anchovy Butter

For use with fish and seafood.

40 g (1½ oz) anchovy fillets
4 tbsp cold milk

100 g (4 oz) butter
1 tsp lemon juice
Freshly ground white pepper

Soak the anchovy fillets in the milk for about 30 minutes, then drain well. Mash the fillets, removing as many bones as possible.

Beat the butter until soft and fluffy, then beat in the anchovy fillets and the lemon juice, adding pepper to taste.

Egg and Onion Butter

For use with fish and vegetables.

100 g (4 oz) salted butter
Yolks of 4 hard-boiled eggs
15 ml (1 tbsp) finely chopped white part of spring onions
Salt
Pepper

Beat the butter until light and fluffy. Press the egg yolks through a sieve. Beat the egg yolks into the butter, then stir in the finely chopped onions. Season with salt and pepper to taste.

Maître d'Hôtel Butter

For use with steaks, chops and fish fillets.

100 g (4 oz) unsalted butter
1 tbsp freshly chopped parsley
5 ml (1 level tsp) salt
1.25 ml (¼ tsp) freshly ground black pepper
1 tsp fresh lemon juice

Beat the butter until soft, then stir in the remaining ingredients. Smooth out the softened mixture to a depth of 3 mm (⅛ in) on non-stick paper and refrigerate until cold.

Cut out shapes using an aspic or small round cutter and

store the butter in the refrigerator or freezer until required. Use the remaining butter trimmings for spreading.

Horseradish Butter

For use with all types of meat.

100 g (4 oz) salted butter
50 g (2 oz) grated horseradish or 1½ tsp horseradish sauce

Beat the butter and horseradish sauce together until creamy. Use for spreading, or pipe rosettes of the butter on to non-stick paper and refrigerate or freeze to use as required.

Walnut Butter

For use with vegetables and fruit.

100 g (4 oz) unsalted butter
40 g (1½ oz) ground walnuts

Beat the butter and the walnuts together until smooth. Use for spreading, or smooth out to a depth of 3mm (⅛ in) on non-stick paper and refrigerate until cold. Cut out shapes with an aspic or small round cutter and store in the refrigerator or the freezer until required. Use the remaining butter trimmings for spreading.

Caper Butter

For use with all fish dishes.

100 g (4 oz) salted butter
15 ml (1 level tbsp) finely chopped capers
Salt
Pepper

Beat the butter until soft and fluffy, then stir in the capers, adding salt and pepper to taste. Spread out to a depth of 6 mm (¼ in) on non-stick paper and cut out coin shapes, using a small round pastry cutter. Store in the refrigerator or freezer until required.

Prawn Butter

For use with fish, egg and chicken dishes.

>   75 g (3 oz) prawns, cooked in their shells
>   100 g (4 oz) unsalted butter
>   Salt
>   Pepper

Remove the heads then pound the unshelled prawns in a pestle and mortar (or use the end of a rolling pin) and rub through a sieve. (The shells will stay in the sieve but the prawns will have a beautiful pink colour.) Beat the butter until soft and fluffy, then mix with the sieved prawns, adding salt and pepper to taste. Put the mixture into a piping bag fitted with a star nozzle and pipe rosettes of the mixture on to non-stick paper. Refrigerate or store in the freezer until required.

Mushroom Butter

For use with fish, meats and poultry.

>   100 g (4 oz) mushrooms
>   100 g (4 oz) unsalted butter
>   2 tsp soured cream
>   White pepper

Cut each stalk off level with the mushroom and wipe the cap. Finely chop the mushroom caps and sauté in 15 g (½ oz) of the butter until soft. Set aside to cool.

Beat the remaining butter until soft and fluffy, then

beat in the cooled mushroom mixture together with the soured cream, seasoning to taste with pepper. Spoon into an attractive dish. Store for 24 hours in the refrigerator in a covered dish.

Garlic Butter

Versatile and suitable for all foods where garlic flavour is preferred.

   4 cloves garlic
   100 g (4 oz) butter
   1 level tsp freshly chopped parsley
   Salt

Peel the garlic, put into a small saucepan, just cover with water and bring to the boil. Drain and set aside to cool.

Crush the cooled garlic in a garlic crusher or pound in between sheets of cling film, using a cleaver or the head of a rolling pin. Place the butter in a bowl and beat until soft and fluffy, then beat in the garlic and the parsley. Season sparingly with salt.

Spread the butter mixture to a depth of 3 mm (⅛ in) on non-stick paper and refrigerate until cold. Using a small round pastry cutter cut out coin shapes of garlic butter and store in a sealed container in the refrigerator or freezer until required. Melt the garlic butter trimmings for basting.

Orange Butter

For use with delicate fish and fruit.

   1 orange
   50 g (2 oz) unsalted butter

Grate the orange rind and squeeze out the juice. Soften the butter and beat in the orange rind and as much juice as the butter will absorb. Form into a sausage shape and wrap, Christmas-cracker fashion, in a sheet of non-stick paper. Freeze until firm or until needed. When required, unwrap the orange butter and slice with a sharp knife, or grate on a coarse grater.

13
Salad Dressings

American Blue Cheese Dressing
Mayonnaise
Green Mayonnaise
Onion and Tarragon Soured-cream Dressing
French Dressing
Thousand Island Dressing
Slimmer's French Dressing

American Blue Cheese Dressing

If you have visited America and enjoyed their salad dressings, then you will like this one. Serve with green salad.

1 small onion, peeled
150 ml (¼ pt) mayonnaise
3 tbsp vegetable oil
1 tbsp tomato ketchup
1 tbsp caster sugar
1 tbsp malt vinegar
1 level tsp French mustard
¼ level tsp paprika
¼ level tsp celery seed
50 g (2 oz) blue cheese (crumbly)
Salt
Pepper

Cut up the onion, then pulp in the liquidizer or food processor. Add all the remaining ingredients except the cheese and process until smooth. Crumble the cheese and stir it into the dressing, then season with salt and pepper to taste. Chill for 2–3 hours before serving.

Makes about 300 ml (½ pt).

Mayonnaise

1 large egg
2.5 ml (½ tsp) French mustard
2.5 ml (½ tsp) salt

2 tsp white wine vinegar
300 ml (½ pt) vegetable oil

Blend the egg, mustard, salt and vinegar in the liquidizer
or food processor for about 10 seconds. While the motor is
still running slowly pour in the oil which should be at room
temperature. Switch off as soon as the mayonnaise has
thickened. (This mayonnaise is not very thick.)

Mayonnaise can be made by hand but the oil must be
added drop by drop until the mixture is well emulsified.
After this the remaining oil can be added more quickly.

Makes 300 ml (½ pt).

Green Mayonnaise

1 bunch watercress
150 ml (¼ pt) thick home-made or bought mayonnaise
1 egg yolk
2 level tbsp freshly chopped chives

Wash the watercress, then pull off the leaves, discarding
the stalks. Pat dry between sheets of kitchen paper.

Put one-third of the mayonnaise into the food processor
or liquidizer. Switch on at full speed, then add the egg
yolk followed by the remaining mayonnaise. When the
mixture has blended and with the motor still running, add
the watercress leaves and the chives. Process until the
leaves are finely chopped and well distributed through the
mayonnaise. Spoon into an attractive serving dish.

Makes about 150 ml (¼ pt).

Onion and Tarragon Soured-cream Dressing

2 tbsp tarragon vinegar
1 small onion, skinned and very finely chopped
1 egg yolk

Pinch dry mustard
Salt
Pepper
150 ml (¼ pt) soured cream
1 level tsp chopped fresh tarragon leaves

Put the vinegar into a small saucepan, add the onion and cook over gentle heat until the vinegar has practically evaporated. Remove from the heat. Beat together the egg yolk, mustard, salt and pepper and stir into the onion. Cook over the lowest possible heat for about 1 minute, stirring vigorously all the time. When the mixture has thickened (take care not to overheat or it will curdle), remove the pan from the heat and stir in the soured cream and the tarragon leaves. Chill for 3 or 4 hours before serving.

Makes just under 300 ml (½ pt).

French Dressing

3 parts good-quality vegetable oil
1 part red or white wine vinegar
Salt
Pepper

Put all the ingredients into a screw-top jar, or empty vinegar bottle, or well-corked wine bottle. Shake before using.

Note: You can flavour the French Dressing to suit your own taste – add a few sprigs of fresh lemon thyme to the bottle, or add a half teaspoon of French or English mustard, or a clove of garlic.

A pinch of sugar will often improve the flavour particularly if you are not using a very good quality salad oil. Try using sesame or walnut oil which gives quite a different taste. Olive oil, traditionally used, is considered by some to be a little on the heavy side.

Thousand Island Dressing

    150 ml (¼ pt) bottled chilli sauce
    2 level tbsp Branston pickle or similar
    2 level tbsp minced onion
    2 level tsp freshly chopped chives
    1 level tsp French mustard
    150 ml (¼ pt) mayonnaise (see page 159)
    150 ml (¼ pt) soured cream
    Salt
    Pepper

Beat all the ingredients thoroughly together, then chill in the refrigerator.

Makes about 450 ml (¾ pt).

Slimmer's French Dressing

    4 level tbsp sunflower oil
    4 level tbsp low fat natural yogurt
    2–3 tbsp fresh lemon juice
    3 tbsp tomato juice
    1 small piece onion
    Salt
    Pepper

Combine all the ingredients thoroughly, cover and set aside for at least 2 hours. Remove the onion, beat the dressing well and use as required.

Makes about 150 ml (¼ pt).

14
Side Salads

Emerald Salad
Oriental Salad
Fruit and Roasted-peanut Salad with Orange Dressing
Waldorf Salad
Tomato Salad
Mushroom Salad
Aubergine Salad
Rice and Sultana Salad
Avocado and Egg Salad
Marinated Cucumber Salad
Coleslaw
Salad Kebabs
Fresh Spinach Salad with Sesame Dressing
Pasta Salad

Emerald Salad

225 g (8 oz) fresh broccoli floretes, washed and drained
225 g (8 oz) fresh cauliflower floretes, washed and drained
225 g (8 oz) cooked peas, fresh or frozen
10–12 spring onions, skinned and finely sliced
1 small clove garlic, skinned and crushed with a pinch of salt
200 ml (7 fl oz) mayonnaise
150 ml (¼ pt) soured cream
Salt and pepper

For garnish
Cress or alfalfa

Cut up the broccoli and cauliflower into bite-sized pieces and mix with the peas. Add the onions well mixed with the garlic. Pour on the mayonnaise and soured cream and mix thoroughly, adding salt and pepper to taste. Cover and refrigerate for several hours.

Just before serving, sprinkle the salad with cress or alfalfa.

Serves about 8, but the recipe can be increased.

Oriental Salad

450 g (1 lb) beansprouts
1 red pepper, cored, seeded and finely chopped
1 tbsp fresh lemon juice

2 tbsp soy sauce
Pepper
Salt

Put the beansprouts into a clean bowl, cover with cold water and leave for 10–15 minutes. Drain thoroughly and dry on kitchen paper or spin in a salad spinner.

Mix the beansprouts in a large salad bowl with the red pepper, lemon juice and soy sauce then add pepper to taste. Add extra salt only if necessary as the soy sauce is salty.

Serves 6–8.

Fruit and Roasted-peanut Salad with Orange Dressing

1 green dessert apple
5 ml (1 tsp) fresh lemon juice
1 tbsp freshly squeezed orange juice
1 tbsp olive oil
1 tight lettuce heart
1 celery stalk
4 radishes
4 spring onions
½ green pepper
25 g (1 oz) dry-roasted peanuts

First prepare the fruit and vegetables. Quarter, core and slice the apple, put into a large salad bowl and sprinkle with the lemon juice and orange juice and add the oil. Finely shred the lettuce, slice the celery thinly and finely chop the radishes, spring onions and green pepper (discarding the core and seeds). Finely chop or grate the peanuts. Add all the ingredients to the bowl and toss until the vegetables and fruit are evenly coated with the dressing.

Serves 6, but the recipe can be increased.

Waldorf Salad

2 red dessert apples
1 celery stalk
25 g (1 oz) chopped walnuts
4 tbsp mayonnaise

For garnish
Cress

Wash and dry the apples, then quarter and core but do not peel. Slice the apples thinly and chop the celery finely. Mix the apples and celery with the nuts and mayonnaise and spoon into a serving dish. Garnish with the cress.

Serves 3–4, but the recipe may be increased.

Tomato Salad

8 firm tomatoes
4 tbsp French dressing
4 tsp red wine
2 level tsp dried basil

Wash the tomatoes and slice thinly, then arrange in overlapping slices in a serving dish. Combine the French dressing with the wine then spoon the mixture over the tomatoes. Sprinkle with basil.
Refrigerate for 2–3 hours before serving.

Serves 6.

Mushroom Salad

100 g (4 oz) button mushrooms
3 tbsp vegetable oil
1 tbsp fresh lemon juice
4 spring onions, white part only, finely chopped

Salt
Pepper

Wipe the mushrooms and cut off the stalks level with
the caps. Discard the stalks. Slice the mushroom caps
finely.

Combine the mushrooms with all the other ingredients
and spoon into a small wooden bowl. Serve as soon as
possible so that the mushrooms retain their texture.

Serves 3–4, but the recipe can be increased.

Aubergine Salad

2 large aubergines, skinned and cut into 1 cm (½ in)
  cubes
1 red pepper, cored and seeded
3 tbsp white wine vinegar
3 tbsp vegetable oil
1 clove garlic, crushed (optional)
Salt
Pepper

Put the aubergine into a saucepan, add water and salt,
then bring to the boil and cook for 5–10 minutes or until
the aubergine is tender. Drain well.

Put the red pepper into a saucepan, add boiling water to
cover and simmer for 3 minutes. Drain and chop into 1 cm
(½ in) squares.

Combine the aubergine and pepper in a salad bowl.
Mix together the vinegar, oil, and garlic, season with salt
and pepper and pour the mixture over the vegetables.
Chill for 1 hour, then stir and taste, adding more seasoning if necessary. Cover and leave in the refrigerator for 12
hours before serving.

Serves 6.

Rice and Sultana Salad

225 g (8 oz) easy-cook long-grain rice
1 level tsp salt
50 g (2 oz) sultanas
3 tbsp vegetable oil
1 tbsp red wine vinegar
1 level tbsp chopped fresh basil
Pepper and salt, to taste
50 g (2 oz) piece cucumber
8 large tomatoes (Moroccan tomatoes are very suitable)
Shredded lettuce

In a large saucepan mix together the rice, salt, sultanas and 600 ml (1 pt) of water. Bring to the boil, stirring once, then reduce the heat. Cover with a lid and simmer for about 15 minutes or until the rice is tender and the liquid is absorbed. (If the rice dries out before it is tender, add a little more boiling water.) Remove the pan from the heat and stir in the oil, vinegar and basil. Season with salt and pepper to taste. Set aside to cool.

Peel and finely dice the cucumber. Cut a slice from the top of each tomato and scoop out the flesh. Sprinkle the inside of each tomato with salt and turn upside down to drain. Mix the diced cucumber with the rice and sultanas and fill the drained tomatoes with the mixture. Replace the lids.

Serve on a bed of shredded lettuce.

Serves 8, but the recipe can be increased.

Avocado and Egg Salad

6 tbsp chopped (white part only) spring onions
1 level tbsp freshly chopped parsley
4 tbsp fresh lemon juice
½ level tsp salt
1 tbsp vegetable oil

3 medium avocados
3 hard-boiled eggs, white part finely chopped, yolks
   sieved
1 level tbsp capers, chopped

For garnish
Shredded lettuce

Mix together the onions, parsley, lemon juice, salt and oil.
   Halve each avocado lengthwise, remove the stone and
peel. Cut the flesh into 0.5–1 cm (¼–½ in) slices and
arrange on a serving dish. Pour the oil mixture over the
avocado slices so that they are completely coated, then
top with the egg and capers. Arrange the shredded lettuce
round the edges of the dish.

Serves 6, but the recipe can be increased.

Marinated Cucumber Salad

This recipe is similar to a pickled type of cucumber and is
very pleasant with meats.

3 large cucumbers
2 level tsp salt
6 tbsp white vinegar
1 level tsp caster sugar
Freshly ground white pepper

Peel the cucumbers and slice thinly. Place in a colander
over a bowl, sprinkle with the salt and leave for at least 30
minutes. Drain thoroughly.
   Put the cucumber into a serving dish. Combine the
vinegar, sugar and 2 tbsp cold water and add a generous
shake of pepper. Pour the mixture over the cucumber
slices, then refrigerate for 3–4 hours.

Serves 6, but the recipe can be increased.

Coleslaw

350 g (12 oz) trimmed white cabbage, coarsely grated
225 g (8 oz) carrots, peeled and finely grated
1 small onion, skinned and finely chopped
300 ml (½ pt) mayonnaise (see page 159)

Mix all the ingredients together thoroughly, then cover and refrigerate overnight. Eat within two days as coleslaw does not keep very well.

Serves 6, but the recipe can be increased.

Salad Kebabs

150 ml (¼ pt) French dressing (see page 161)
Selection fresh herbs, chopped
6 firm tomatoes, lightly pricked with a thin skewer or cocktail stick
½ cucumber, peeled, quartered lengthwise and cut into thick chunks
12 button mushrooms, stalks removed
12 bottled pearl onions
1 × 397 g (14 oz) can artichoke bottoms, drained and quartered
1 green pepper, cored, seeded and cut into 2.5 cm (1 in) pieces
1 red pepper, cored, seeded, and cut into 2.5 cm (1 in) pieces
6 cauliflower floretes, washed
6 tiny new potatoes, boiled in their skins

Make up the French dressing and divide between two deep narrow bowls, putting 1–2 tablespoons of different chopped herbs into each. Add four or five varieties of vegetables to each bowl and toss to coat. Cover and refrigerate, stirring occasionally, for 2 hours.

Thread the vegetables alternately on to flat-sided skewers. They are now ready to serve.

Serves 6, but the recipe can be increased or decreased. If you are making less, reduce the quantity of vegetables but not the amount of French dressing and herbs.

Fresh Spinach Salad with Sesame Dressing

450 g (1 lb) fresh young spinach
1 celery stalk, finely chopped
1 small onion, skinned and finely chopped
1 clove garlic, crushed
2 level tbsp sesame seeds
3 tbsp vegetable oil
1 tbsp fresh lemon juice
Salt and pepper, to taste

Wash the spinach, tear or cut the leaves completely away from the stalks and press between sheets of kitchen paper to dry. Pile the leaves on top of one another and shred coarsely with a sharp knife. Just before serving, mix in all the other ingredients, adding salt and pepper to taste.

Serves 6, but the recipe can be increased.

Pasta Salad

100 g (4 oz) tiny pasta shells
1 tsp vegetable oil
4 level tbsp mango chutney
8 level tbsp mayonnaise
2 level tbsp sultanas
4 level tbsp single cream
2 celery stalks, finely sliced
¼ green pepper, diced
100 g (4 oz) button mushrooms, sliced

Cook the pasta in a large pan of boiling salted water to which the vegetable oil has been added. Rinse in cold water and drain thoroughly.

Mix all the remaining ingredients together in a salad bowl, add the pasta and toss thoroughly.

Serves 6, but the recipe can be increased.

15
Vegetables

Duchesse Potatoes
Almond, Sesame Seed and Carrot Noodles
Garlic Beans and Mushrooms
Glazed Sweet Potatoes
Courgettes with Fresh Herbs
Homely Baked Beans
Bavarian Red Cabbage
Corn Fritters
Plain Boiled Rice
Saffron Rice
Egg Fried Rice
Vegetable Pilau
Dolmades

Vegetables

Although it would be a lovely thought to be able to cook a large selection of dishes on the barbecue, it really is not practical unless you have more than one barbecue or have a specially built large barbecue to cater for a big party. Quite a number of vegetable dishes can be cooked in the conventional oven and kept hot without deterioration while others can be quickly reheated on the grid of the barbecue; of course you can always reheat in the microwave oven provided you use the appropriate containers.

Duchesse Potatoes

These can be prepared in advance, then baked when required.

    1½ lb potatoes, peeled
    40 g (1½ oz) butter
    2 tbsp milk
    1 egg, beaten
    Salt
    Pepper

Boil the potatoes until soft (about 20 minutes) then drain and return them to the saucepan, stirring over the lowest possible heat to dry out all moisture. Press the potatoes through a sieve (do not use a food blender) then beat in the butter, 1 tbsp of the milk and about three-quarters of the egg. Season with salt and pepper to taste.

Check that the mixture is soft enough to pipe, then put it into a large piping bag fitted with a 1 cm (½ in) star nozzle. Pipe twelve potato pyramids on to a baking sheet which is either greased or lined with non-stick paper. Blend together the remaining milk and egg and brush this over the potatoes.

Bake in a pre-heated oven 190°C (375°F) Gas 5 for 20–30 minutes or until the potatoes are golden brown.

Serves 6, but the recipe can be increased.

Almond, Sesame Seed and Carrot Noodles

Serve this dish with Korean Sliced Beef, meatballs or lamb kebabs.

30 ml (2 level tbsp) sesame seeds
1 medium onion, peeled and finely chopped
50 g (2 oz) butter
50 g (2 oz) mushrooms, chopped
2 large carrots, scraped and grated
30 ml (2 tbsp) soy sauce
15 ml (1 tbsp) sherry
Salt
Pepper
450 g (1 lb) ribbon noodles

Topping
30 ml (2 level tbsp) grated Parmesan cheese

For serving
50 g (2 oz) flaked almonds

First brown the almonds and the sesame seeds separately in the oven or under the grill, taking care with the latter as sesame seeds burn quickly.

Sauté the onion in the butter, then add the mushrooms and carrots and cook for a further 5 minutes. Remove the pan from the heat and stir in the sesame seeds, soy sauce and sherry and season to taste with salt and pepper.

Cook and drain the noodles and add them to the cooked vegetables, then spoon the whole into a double-thickness-foil or metal dish. Sprinkle over the Parmesan cheese. Place the dish in a pre-heated oven 180°C (350°F) Gas 4, and bake for 10 minutes; alternatively cook on the grid in a covered barbecue.

Sprinkle with the almonds before serving.

Serves 6, but the recipe can be increased.

Garlic Beans and Mushrooms

Serve with burgers, chops, sausages or roast meat.

350 g (¾ lb) French or thin runner beans
100 g (4 oz) mushrooms, sliced
2 celery stalks, finely sliced
4–5 spring onions, skinned and sliced
1 level tbsp dried parsley
½ tsp dried oregano
5 tbsp white wine vinegar
3 tbsp vegetable oil
2 cloves garlic, finely crushed
Salt
Pepper

Cook the beans, then drain thoroughly. Return them to the saucepan and mix in the remaining ingredients. Cook for 5 minutes, then remove the pan from the heat, cover with the lid and leave for 1–2 hours for the flavours to develop.

Just before serving, reheat and pour into a dish which will be suitable to keep hot on the barbecue.

Serves 4–6, but the recipe can be increased.

Glazed Sweet Potatoes

    900 g (2 lb) sweet potatoes
    50 g (2 oz) demerara sugar
    ½ level tsp ground cinnamon
    ½ level tsp ground nutmeg
    Juice of 2 oranges
    50 g (2 oz) butter

Peel and slice the potatoes thinly. Mix together the sugar, cinnamon, nutmeg and orange juice. In a large metal casserole or deep foil dish make layers of the potatoes, dabs of butter and the sauce, finishing with a layer of butter. Cover with a lid and bake in a pre-heated oven at 200°C (400°F) Gas 6 for about 1½ hours, basting occasionally, until the potatoes are soft and coated in a thick syrup. Serve straight from the oven or transfer the dish to the barbecue.

Serves 6, but the recipe can be increased.

Courgettes with Fresh Herbs

    675 g (1½ lb) even-sized courgettes
    2 bay leaves, crushed or snipped with sharp scissors
    1 rounded tbsp freshly chopped parsley
    1 rounded tsp tarragon leaves
    1 rounded tsp fresh lemon thyme leaves
    ½ level tsp salt
    ¼ level tsp freshly ground white pepper
    1 clove garlic, crushed
    2 tbsp fresh lemon juice
    4 tbsp vegetable oil

Top and tail the courgettes and cut them into 1 cm (½ in) slices. Put them into a large bowl and add all the other ingredients. Cover and leave for 5–6 hours in a cool place, stirring once or twice.

To cook, either transfer to a saucepan or put into a metal casserole, adding 2–3 tablespoons of water. Cover and cook for 8 to 10 minutes over medium heat on the cooker or over the hot coals on the barbecue, shaking the pan from time to time.

Serves 6, but the recipe can be increased.

Homely Baked Beans

350 g (¾ lb) dried haricot beans
1 level tsp salt
2 garlic cloves, peeled and crushed
3 tbsp vegetable oil
1 × 227 g (8 oz) can tomatoes
30 ml (2 level tbsp) tomato purée
½ level tsp dried basil
Pepper and salt, to taste

Put the beans into a large saucepan or bowl, cover with plenty of cold water and leave overnight. Drain and rinse thoroughly.

To cook, put the beans into a large heavy-based saucepan, cover with cold water and bring to the boil. Simmer for 1 hour, then stir in the salt and cook for a further 5 minutes. Drain thoroughly.

Dry the saucepan, then sauté the garlic in the oil for 2–3 minutes. Stir in the cooked beans, the contents of the can of tomatoes, the tomato purée, basil, and pepper to taste. Cover with the lid and simmer over gentle heat for about 30 minutes, or until the mixture thickens. Season to taste with salt and more pepper if necessary. Pour into a metal or foil lidded casserole and keep hot on the side of the barbecue.

Serves 6–8, but the recipe can be increased, in which case it will not take very much longer to cook.

Bavarian Red Cabbage

To be served with roast pork.

  1 small red cabbage
  2 rashers streaky bacon, rinds removed
  1 medium onion, finely chopped
  2 rounded tbsp demerara sugar
  1 tbsp vinegar
  2 medium cooking apples, peeled, cored and sliced
  Salt
  Pepper

Cut the cabbage into quarters and remove the fibrous stalks. Shred the cabbage finely.

Chop the bacon and put into a saucepan with the onions. Cook gently over medium heat for 5 minutes or until the bacon is cooked and the onion is soft. Stir the cabbage into the onion mixture and add the sugar, vinegar and apples. Season with salt and pepper, cover tightly with a lid and cook over minimum heat for about 1 hour, stirring occasionally, or until the cabbage is soft.

Serves 6, but the recipe can be increased.

Note: If you are going to keep this hot on the barbecue, the dish must be kept well away from the heat as the cabbage burns easily.

Corn Fritters

  100 g (4 oz) frozen sweetcorn kernels
  75 g (3 oz) plain flour
  Pinch salt
  1 egg, lightly beaten
  2 tbsp water
  2 tbsp milk
  Salt

Pepper
Pinch nutmeg
Equal quantities of oil and butter for frying

Cook the corn kernels, drain and leave to cool.

Sift the flour and salt into a mixing bowl and beat in the egg, water and milk to form a thick smooth batter. Season to taste with salt and pepper and add the nutmeg.

Heat a little oil and butter in a heavy-based frying pan and, when hot, add the corn mixture, a tablespoon at a time, allowing the fritters to spread out. As soon as the fritters are brown underneath, turn them over to cook the other side.

When all the fritters are cooked, drain and keep hot either in the oven or replace in the cleaned frying pan and keep hot on the sides of the barbecue grid.

Makes about 12.

Rice
Boiled or steamed rice may be cooked by any method that you are used to, but do bear the following points in mind. If the rice has to be kept hot, it is better to under- rather than to over-cook, and to leave a little liquid in the pan. Keep the rice hot in a lidded casserole in a cool oven.

If rice is to be reheated or used in another dish where cooked rice is required, do not wrap it in foil or you will find that the foil has become considerably pitted and little bits adhere to the rice. I understand that this is not dangerous, but it is certainly not appetizing.

You cannot cover dishes with cling film if they are to be kept warm in the traditional oven, but it is suitable for use in the microwave, which is superb for reheating rice just when you need it. Put the rice into dishes which are suitable for use in the microwave oven and partially cover with cling film before reheating. If you have rice stored in the freezer and want to reheat by microwave, there is no need to add extra liquid; however, if you are reheating cooled rice in the microwave, add one or two teaspoons of water.

Rice can also be reheated on top of the cooker by one of the following methods: (1) Place the rice in a metal colander over a pan of boiling water, covering the colander with the saucepan lid. (2) Bring a large saucepan of water to the boil, drop in the rice grains, bring back to the boil, then strain and serve at once.

Obviously, the easiest way of serving rice at a barbecue is to have the rice ready cooked; then it can be tossed in melted butter for reheating.

Rice now comes in so many forms that it is difficult to give exact quantities, so follow the instructions on the packet. Ordinary long-grain rice takes about 15 minutes to cook. As a general guide allow 40–50 g (1½–2 oz) raw rice per person – it trebles in volume and weight when cooked.

Saffron Rice

Cook the rice in the usual way, adding 1/8th tsp powdered saffron for every 225 g (8 oz) rice. When the rice is cooked, fork in 25 g (1 oz) butter.

Egg Fried Rice

225 g (8 oz) long-grain rice, freshly cooked and warm
1 tbsp vegetable oil
1 tbsp soy sauce
3 eggs
Vegetable oil for frying

Put the rice into a saucepan and stir in the oil and soy sauce. Heat gently until the rice is hot enough to serve. Cover the pan and switch off the heat.

Beat the eggs, pour into a large lightly oiled frying pan and cook until set. Turn the omelette over to lightly brown the other side. Slide it on to a board, roll up tightly Swiss-roll fashion, then cut into very thin strips. Mix the egg into the rice. Spoon the mixture into a heated metal casserole or serve from the saucepan.

Serves 6, but the recipe can be increased.

Vegetable Pilau

75 g (3 oz) butter
350 g (12 oz) long-grain rice, rinsed and drained
75 g (3 oz) hazelnuts, finely chopped
900 ml (1½ pt) chicken stock
1 level tsp salt
1 level tsp ground cardamom
1 level tsp ground turmeric
50 g (2 oz) sultanas
½ red pepper, diced
½ green pepper, diced
4 tbsp frozen peas

Melt the butter in a large heavy-based saucepan, then stir in the rice and nuts. Cook, stirring continuously for about 3 minutes or until the rice and nuts turn a light golden colour. Add all the remaining ingredients, stir thoroughly and bring to the boil. Reduce the heat, cover tightly with the lid and cook gently for 15 minutes. Do not remove the lid during this cooking time. Remove the lid, test the rice; if the rice is not yet cooked but the liquid has evaporated, add a little more water. On the other hand, if the rice is cooked but there is a large amount of liquid left, raise the heat and boil quickly to evaporate.

Turn the mixture into a serving dish and serve at once. If the rice is to be kept hot, it is better to have it a little more moist and keep it covered in a lidded casserole in a cool oven.

Serves 6 to 8, but the recipe can be increased.

Dolmades

Dolmades are soft vine leaves stuffed usually with flavoured rice alone but you can add some chopped chicken
if you prefer.

50 g (2 oz) long-grain rice
½ level tsp dried dill weed
2 spring onions, peeled and finely chopped
Few sprigs fresh mint
Salt
Pepper
4 tbsp olive oil
12 canned vine leaves

Put the rice, dill weed, onions and mint into a saucepan of
boiling salted water and cook until the rice is tender.
Drain, remove the mint and season the rice with salt and
pepper. Stir in the oil. Leave to cool.

Place a heaped teaspoon of the cooled mixture in the
centre of each vine leaf and roll up from the stem end,
folding in the sides of the leaf to enclose the rice and form
packets.

Pack the dolmades in a single layer in the bottom of a
heavy-based saucepan, just cover the packets with water
and put a plate on top of them so that they stay flat while
being cooked.

Cook over gentle heat for 45 minutes. Remove the
dolmades carefully from the pan with a slotted spoon and
serve hot or cold.

Serves 6, but the recipe can be increased.

16
Soups

Matsutake Soup
Chinatown Soup
Smooth Spinach Soup
Three-bean Soup
Cream of Tomato Soup
Lettuce Soup
Iced Cucumber Soup
Beetroot Soup
Punjabi Curry Soup
Gazpacho

Matsutake Soup

6 open flat mushrooms, wiped and finely shredded
100 g (4 oz) skinned and boned chicken breast, cubed
50 g (2 oz) cooked shelled prawns or raw prawns if available, chopped
900 ml (1½ pt) chicken stock
2.5 ml (½ tsp) salt
15 ml (1 tbsp) light soya sauce
1.25 ml (¼ tsp) monosodium glutamate
50 g (2 oz) spinach leaves, finely chopped
Juice of 1 lemon

Combine the ingredients, except the spinach and lemon juice, in a large heavy saucepan. Bring to the boil, cover and simmer lidded for 20 minutes. Skim, then stir in the spinach and lemon juice. Replace the lid, then remove from the heat and serve immediately. (If the pan is suitable it can be briefly rested on the barbecue grill.)

Serves 4–6, but the amounts may be increased to serve larger numbers.

Chinatown Soup

1.25 litre (2¼ pt) well-flavoured chicken stock
1 × 100 g (4 oz) boned chicken breast, shredded
25 g (1 oz) piece red pepper, sliced very thinly
50 g (2 oz) bamboo shoots, thinly sliced
50 g (2 oz) water chestnuts, very thinly sliced
50 g (2 oz) instant soup noodles or vermicelli

Salt
Pepper

Put the stock into a large saucepan and bring to the boil. Add the shredded chicken and simmer without a lid for 5 minutes. Stir in the red pepper, bamboo shoots and water chestnuts and, without covering, simmer for 15 minutes, stirring occasionally. Finally, add the noodles and simmer for a further 5 minutes, then adjust the seasoning if necessary.

Serves 9–12.

Note: If you use the instant soup noodles, don't add the stock sachet as this alters the flavour of the soup. The bamboo and water chestnuts come canned and any left-overs can be used in stir fry dishes, salads or casseroles.

Smooth Spinach Soup

25 g (1 oz) butter
1 medium onion, skinned and finely sliced
350 g (¾ lb) potatoes, peeled, quartered and sliced
40 g (1½ oz) flour
450 g (1 lb) frozen chopped or pelleted spinach
Salt
Pepper
Nutmeg
6 tbsp single cream
½ tsp fresh lemon juice

Melt the butter in a large saucepan, then stir in the onion and potatoes. Cover with a lid and cook over medium heat, shaking the pan from time to time until the vegetables are glossy. Stir in the flour, then add the spinach and 900 ml (1½ pt) water.

Bring to the boil, then season with salt, pepper and nutmeg. Simmer over gentle heat until the potatoes are soft. Blend in the liquidizer, then reheat the soup. Adjust the seasoning and stir in the single cream and lemon juice just before serving. Add extra boiling water or stock if the soup is too thick.

Serves 8–10, but the recipe can be increased.

Three-bean Soup

  1 × 220 g (7¾ oz) can butter beans, drained
  1 × 284 g (10 oz) can broad beans, drained
  1 × 440 g (15½ oz) can baked beans, undrained
  1 medium onion, thinly sliced
  2 level tsp chilli compound seasoning
  2 tbsp tomato purée
  1 beef Oxo cube, or vegetable stock cube, crumbled

Combine all the ingredients in a large saucepan. Add 450 ml (¾ pt) water, then bring to the boil. Simmer without a lid for ½ hour, stirring occasionally.

Serves 8, but the recipe can be stretched to serve 12 by the addition of extra water, tomato purée and a stock cube.

Cream of Tomato Soup

  50 g (2 oz) butter
  50 g (2 oz) flour
  300 ml (½ pt) milk
  1 × 800 g (1 lb 12 oz) can tomatoes
  1 level tsp bay leaf powder
  Salt
  Pepper

Melt the butter in a large saucepan and stir in the flour. Gradually add the milk, beating continuously until the sauce thickens. Add the tomatoes and their juice, crushing them with a potato masher or fork, and stir in the bay leaf powder. Cook until the mixture comes back to the boil. Season to taste with salt and pepper. Blend the soup in the liquidizer, then pour through a sieve to remove the pips.

Serves 6, but the recipe can be increased.

Lettuce Soup

   1 round lettuce
   1 small onion, skinned and finely chopped
   40 g (1½ oz) butter
   450 ml (¾ pt) well-flavoured chicken stock
   Pinch sugar
   Pinch ground nutmeg
   450 ml (¾ pt) milk
   Green food colouring

Wash the lettuce, separate the leaves and discard any thick stems. Put the lettuce leaves into a large saucepan of boiling salted water. Bring back to the boil and simmer for 5 minutes. Rinse thoroughly in a colander under cold running water, then drain and shred (kitchen scissors are useful for this).

Using the same saucepan, sauté the onion in the butter for 3–4 minutes or until the onion is soft. Add the shredded lettuce and the chicken stock, the sugar and nutmeg, cover with the lid, bring to simmering point and cook for 15–20 minutes.

Blend the soup in the liquidizer. Return the soup to the saucepan, stir in the milk and bring back to boiling point. (A few drops of green food colouring greatly enhance the colour but this is not essential.) Serve the soup hot or cold.

Serves 6, but the recipe can be increased.

Iced Cucumber Soup

25 g (1 oz) butter
1 small onion, skinned and chopped
1½ large cucumbers, washed and dried
600 ml (1 pt) well-flavoured chicken stock
150 ml (¼ pt) milk
Salt
White pepper

In a large saucepan melt the butter, add the onion and cook until soft. Cut the unpeeled cucumber into small pieces, add to the onion mixture and sauté gently for about 3 minutes until the vegetables are completely coated in the butter. Add half the stock and bring to the boil. Cover with the lid, reduce the heat and simmer for about 15 minutes. Blend the soup in the liquidizer, about a third at a time, then return the soup to the saucepan.

Stir in the milk and the remaining stock. Bring back to the boil, then pour into a tureen. Cover and leave to cool, then chill in the refrigerator. Adjust the seasoning before serving.

Serves 6–8.

Beetroot Soup

450 g (1 lb) raw beetroot, peeled and grated
100 g (4 oz) carrots, peeled and grated
100 g (4 oz) potatoes, peeled and grated
1 tbsp red wine vinegar
1 litre (1¾ pt) well-flavoured chicken stock
450 ml (¾ pt) tomato juice
Salt
Pepper
150 ml (¼ pt) soured cream

Combine the ingredients, except the soured cream, in a large saucepan. Bring to the boil, then cover with a lid and

B.C.–H

simmer for 45 minutes. Stir in the cream just before serving. Serve hot or cold.

Serves 12.

Punjabi Curry Soup

    3 medium onions, skinned and finely sliced
    3 tbsp oil
    4 level tsp mild curry paste
    3 green peppers, cored, seeded and finely sliced
    1 litre (1¾ pt) water or chicken stock
    1 × 450 g (1 lb) carton natural yogurt
    Salt
    Pepper

Fry the onions in the oil until soft and just brown, then stir in the curry paste. Add the green peppers, then the water or chicken stock. Bring to the boil and simmer until the peppers are soft – about 30 minutes.

Blend the soup in the liquidizer, leave to cool, then stir in the yogurt and season to taste with salt and pepper.

Chill in the refrigerator and serve cold.

Serves 10–12, but the recipe can be increased.

Gazpacho

    900 g (2 lb) ripe tomatoes
    1 large onion, peeled
    1 medium cucumber, unpeeled
    2 large green peppers, cored and seeded
    30 ml (2 tbsp) tomato purée
    2 tbsp vegetable oil
    2 tbsp red wine vinegar
    1 tbsp sherry
    Few drops Tabasco sauce

1.25 ml (¼ tsp) celery salt
Salt
Pepper

For serving
Paprika croûtons

Put the tomatoes in a large bowl, cover with boiling water and leave for 5 minutes or until they begin to soften. Blend the tomatoes, half the onion, half the cucumber and 1 green pepper in the liquidizer or food processor. Press through a sieve into a tureen to remove the tomato seeds and skins. Finely chop the remaining onion, cucumber and pepper and stir into the purée. Chill for 2–3 hours and serve topped with paprika croûtons (see below).

Serves 6, but the recipe can be increased.

Note: To make the croûtons: cut crustless bread into small dice, shallow fry in a mixture of oil and butter to which has been added a teaspoon of paprika, then drain thoroughly.

Croûtons invariably make soup more appetizing and give a touch of class. Serve them hot and freshly made with hot soup and cold with chilled soups.

17
Desserts

Rumtopf
Fresh Berry Crumble
Strawberry Syllabub
Lemon Mousse
Treacle Tart
Profiteroles with Chocolate Sauce
Melon Basket
Raspberries with Strawberry Sauce
Baklava
Gulabjamun
Sliced Oranges in Ginger Syrup
Sliced Fresh Mango with Limes
Pineapple Rings with Kirsch
Deep-dish Apple Pie

Rumtopf

Summer fruits or frozen soft fruits including strawberries, raspberries, redcurrants, pitted cherries, loganberries, blackcurrants, blackberries, apricots, pineapple, pitted plums, nectarines, mango, seedless grapes
Granulated sugar
Rum
Brandy

Using a large lidded earthenware pot layer the fruits about 2.5 cm (1 in) deep with an equal depth of sugar, soaking generously with rum and a little brandy after each addition. Continue adding layers of fruit and sugar and topping up with the spirits, each time a new fruit comes into the shops. You can do this over a period of several weeks but you must make sure that the fruit is completely covered with sugar and spirits. Keep the lid on tightly and store for at least one month before using.

The flavour improves with keeping and is best at around six months although it can be kept for much longer. During long keeping it might be necessary to top up with extra sugar and spirits.

You can also serve this dessert in autumn or winter and include some frozen fruits, but beware – it is very intoxicating. Serve only small portions topped with plenty of freshly whipped cream – do not use ice cream as you may find that it is too sweet.

Make as large a quantity as your pot will take.

Fresh Berry Crumble

    200 g (8 oz) self-raising flour
    100 g (4 oz) butter or margarine
    100 g (4 oz) caster sugar
    450 g (1 lb) strawberries, washed and hulled
    350 g (¾ lb) raspberries, whole
    300 ml (½ pt) double cream

Sift the flour into a mixing bowl, rub in the butter until the mixture resembles breadcrumbs, then stir in the sugar. Spread the mixture out in a thin layer in a roasting dish or baking tray and bake in a pre-heated oven 190°C (375°F) Gas 5 for about 10–15 minutes or until golden brown (the mixture should be stirrable). Leave to cool.

Reserve six whole strawberries and slice the remainder. Leave the raspberries whole. Whip the cream until soft peaks form, then mix with both fruits. Using six straight-sided glasses or sundae dishes, make alternate layers of fruit and crumble, finishing with a layer of crumble. Top each portion with a single strawberry.

Serves 6, but the recipe can be doubled by using two roasting dishes to bake the crumble mix.

Strawberry Syllabub

This recipe is also suitable for freezing provided that when required sufficient time is allowed for thawing.

    1 lb strawberries, washed and hulled
    4 egg whites
    225 g (8 oz) caster sugar
    300 ml (½ pt) double cream
    8 tbsp sweet white wine

For decoration
    Sliced strawberries

Purée the strawberries in the liquidizer or food processor, or press through a sieve. Put the egg whites into a grease-free bowl and whisk until stiff peaks form. Gradually add the strawberry purée and sugar alternately to the egg-white mixture and whisk again until thick. Add the cream and wine, whisking vigorously until the mixture is well blended.

Pour into individual wine or sundae glasses and leave for several hours in a cool place. If you choose to use the refrigerator, place the syllabubs on the lowest shelf. Just before serving, decorate with thin slices of whole straw-berries cut lengthwise. This is a separated syllabub in which the strawberry liquid is meant to sink to the bottom.

Serves 8, but the recipe may be increased.

Lemon Mousse

3 eggs plus 2 egg yolks
100 g (4 oz) caster sugar
15 g (½ oz) (1 sachet) powdered gelatine
Juice of 1 lemon
1 × 200 ml (7 fl oz) can frozen concentrated orange juice, thawed
150 ml (¼ pt) double cream, whipped

Whisk the eggs, extra yolks and sugar together until thick and smooth, when a fork drawn through the mixture leaves a channel.

Mix the gelatine with the lemon juice in a small bowl and stand the bowl (but do not immerse) in a pan of boiling water. Stir the gelatine until dissolved, then carefully remove the bowl from the water.

Pour the dissolved gelatine from a height on to the egg mixture and beat vigorously. Add the orange juice and continue beating until the mixture is well blended, then fold in the cream.

Pour into individual glasses or one large bowl and leave until set. Setting will be quicker if the bowl or glasses are refrigerated, but do not freeze.

Serves 6, but the recipe can be increased.

Treacle Tart

100 g (4 oz) soft margarine
1 tbsp ice-cold water
175 g (6 oz) plain flour
Pinch salt

For the filling
3 rounded tbsp fresh breadcrumbs
grated rind and juice of ½ orange
4 tbsp golden syrup

To make the pastry, put the margarine, water and 2 tbsp flour in a mixing bowl and beat until well blended. Stir in the remaining flour and the salt and knead to form a firm dough. Roll out on a floured surface and fit into a 175 cm (7 in) fluted flan dish. Line the pastry with greaseproof paper and baking beans and bake in a preheated hot oven 200°C (400°F) Gas 6 for 15 minutes. Remove the paper and baking beans from the pastry after another 5 minutes but don't turn off the heat.

Meanwhile mix the breadcrumbs, orange rind, juice and golden syrup thoroughly together. Spoon the filling into the flan dish, spreading out the mixture over the warm pastry. Return the flan dish to the oven and bake for a further 15–25 minutes, or until the filling thickens. Serve warm or cold with whipped cream or custard.

Serves 5, but if you wish to increase the recipe, pre-cook several pastry cases and proportionately increase the filling ingredients which can be mixed in one batch and divided up accordingly.

Profiteroles with Chocolate Sauce

50 g (2 oz) butter or margarine
150 ml (¼ pt) water
65 g (2½ oz) plain flour
Pinch salt } sieved together
2 eggs

For the filling
150 ml (¼ pt) double cream, whipped

For the chocolate sauce
100 g (4 oz) plain dessert chocolate
1 × 150 g (6 oz) can evaporated milk

Put the butter in a medium saucepan over low heat, add the water and bring to the boil. Immediately remove from the heat and add the flour all at once, beating thoroughly. Return the saucepan briefly to the heat and beat vigorously until the mixture becomes shiny and leaves the sides of the pan. Do not overbeat.

Leave the mixture to cool slightly, then beat the eggs in, one at a time. As each egg is added the mixture will appear to curdle but further beating will make sure that the eggs are properly incorporated. The pastry should be more like a heavy batter than a dough.

Place teaspoons of the mixture, well spaced out, on a greased baking sheet (or line the sheet with non-stick paper) and bake in a preheated hot oven 200°C (400°F) Gas 6 for 15 minutes. Quickly turn the baking sheet round or change its position. Reduce the temperature to 190°C (375°F) Gas 5, and bake for a further 15–20 minutes or until the buns are well risen and crisp on the outside.

Cool the buns on a wire rack, then make a slit in each and fill with whipped cream. Pile on to a serving dish.

To make the sauce, break the chocolate into pieces and put into a bowl over a pan of hot water, making sure that the water does not touch the base of the bowl. Stir in the milk and beat thoroughly. Pour the sauce over the choux buns just before serving.

Serves 4 (makes about 12), but the recipe can be doubled – the maximum that can be mixed at any one time.

Melon Basket

1 green melon
small amount of firm colourful fruit such as cherries; fresh pineapple; satsuma segments; apples; firm peaches, skinned; ripe gooseberries, hulled
1–2 tbsp caster sugar
1 tbsp liqueur such as Grand Marnier

Remove a small slice from the base of the melon so that the fruit will stand steadily. Cut a lid from the melon about 5 cm (2 in) in depth. Remove the melon seeds. Using a teaspoon or potato baller, cut out balls of the fruit but do not cut too close to the walls. Mix the melon balls with other fruits adding the sugar and liqueur. Using a sharp knife zig-zag the rim of the melon basket and fill the melon with the fruit.

To make an attractive handle, cut the centre strip from the top of the melon and shave away the surplus flesh. Cut out a V shape at either end of the strip so that it will dovetail against either side of the melon basket, and place in position. Rub the outside of the melon with a little oil to give it a shine and arrange it on a platter surrounded by any surplus fruit. Chill before serving.

Serves 6–8, but you can prepare as many melons as you like.

Raspberries with Strawberry Sauce

450 g (1 lb) raspberries, fresh or frozen
350 g (12 oz) fresh strawberries, hulled
Sugar to taste
Stiffly whipped fresh cream
2 tbsp flaked almonds

Put the raspberries into individual tall glasses. Liquidize the strawberries with sugar to taste. Pour the puréed strawberries over the raspberries, then top with whipped cream and flaked almonds. If the cream is sufficiently stiff, you can keep the desserts in the refrigerator for 1–2 hours before serving.

Serves 6, but the recipe can be increased.

Baklava

450 g (1 lb) phyllo or uncooked strudel leaves (obtainable from specialist Greek shops)
225 g (8 oz) unsalted butter, melted

For the syrup

225 g (8 oz) sugar
2 generous tbsp clear honey
2 tsp fresh lemon juice
1 tbsp orange juice

For the filling

175 g (6 oz) walnuts, finely chopped
100 g (4 oz) blanched almonds, finely chopped
½ level tsp ground cinnamon
½ level tsp ground nutmeg
50 g (2 oz) caster sugar

To make the syrup, dissolve the sugar in 150 ml (¼ pt) water over gentle heat, then stir in the honey and fruit juices and bring to the boil. Reduce the heat and simmer for 3–4 minutes or until the syrup will coat the back of a spoon. Cool and refrigerate.

To prepare the filling, just mix all the ingredients together.

Heat the oven to 160°C (325°F) Gas 3. Brush the base and sides of a deep roasting tin with butter, lay in two of the pastry leaves (which should be the size of the roasting tin) and brush these with butter. Repeat this process until you have used up half the pastry. Sprinkle with about two-thirds of the filling. Layer and butter another four phyllo or strudel leaves, and cover with the remainder of the filling. Layer and butter the remaining pastry and pour any surplus butter over the top. Using a sharp knife and cutting through the top layers only, criss-cross the pastry to mark out diamond-shaped portions.

Place the tin in the oven and bake for 30 minutes, then raise the oven temperature to 230°C (450°F) Gas 8 and bake for a further 12–15 minutes or until the pastry is golden and puffy.

Remove the tin from the oven, pour the syrup over the pastry and cut through into separate portions but leave in the tin until the syrup is well soaked in and the pastry cool. Serve from the tin.

Makes up to 30 pieces, depending on their size.

Gulabjamun

16 level tbsp full-cream powdered milk
4 level tbsp self-raising flour
4–6 tbsp milk
Oil for deep frying

For the syrup
450 g (1 lb) sugar
450 ml (¾ pt) water

2 tbsp rose water (or few drops rose-flavouring food
   essence)

Sift together the powdered milk and flour, then mix in the
milk a little at a time to form a stiff dough. Knead until
smooth, then divide the mixture into walnut-sized balls
and fry at 180°C (370°F). The oil must not be too hot or
the outside of the balls will turn dark brown before the
inside has started to cook. The gulabjamun are ready
when golden brown. Drain on kitchen paper.

To make the syrup, heat the sugar and the water in a
heavy-based frying pan until the sugar has dissolved.
Bring to the boil and cook for 3–4 minutes, or until the
syrup thickens slightly. Stir in the rose water or rose-
flavouring essence.

Add the gulabjamun to the syrup, remove the pan from
the heat, cover with the lid and leave to steep for 10–15
minutes. Serve the gulabjamun warm or cold with a little
of the syrup.

Serves 6, but the recipe can be increased.

Sliced Oranges in Ginger Syrup

   3 large oranges
   1 small can mandarin oranges
   4 or 5 pieces crystallized ginger

To prepare the oranges, you need a sharp knife and a
chopping board. Cut off the top and bottom of each
orange so that the flesh is exposed, and the orange will
stand steadily on the board. Remove the pith and peel by
cutting downwards closely following the contours of the
flesh. Slice the oranges thinly and put into a serving
dish. Liquidize the contents of the can of mandarins
together with the crystallized ginger. Pour the resulting

syrup over the oranges and chill for several hours before serving.

Serves 6, but the recipe can be increased.

Sliced Fresh Mango with Limes

    4 ripe mangoes
    lettuce leaves
    Juice of 2 fresh limes

Have a bowl of cold water beside you when you peel the mangoes as it tends to be a messy business. After peeling, slice the mango flesh lengthwise close to the stone. Divide into individual portions and arrange on lettuce leaves on one large dish, or on separate small dishes. Sprinkle with the lime juice and chill until required.

Serves 6, but the recipe can be increased.

Pineapple Rings with Kirsch

I have not given specific quantities in this recipe as it very much depends upon the size of pineapple that you buy.

    1 ripe pineapple, peeled, pitted and cut into rings
    2–4 tbsp Kirsch
    Icing sugar
    Butter
    Halved glacé cherries
    Chopped angelica

Sprinkle the pineapple rings with the Kirsch and dust generously with the icing sugar. When you are ready to serve, heat 25 g (1 oz) butter in a large heavy-based frying pan over hot coals. Add the pineapple rings to the melted butter, then turn them over so that they are coated on both sides. When the pineapple rings are warm, serve topped with the glacé cherries and chopped angelica.

Deep-dish Apple Pie

900 g (2 lb) cooking apples
150 g (5 oz) demerara sugar
Juice and rind of 1 lemon
⅛ tsp ground cloves
Knob of butter
Shortcrust pastry made from 250 g (8 oz) flour and 125 g (4 oz) chosen fat, or use 1 × 350 g (12 oz) pack ready-made shortcrust pastry

To glaze
Beaten egg and sugar

First prepare the fruit. Peel, core and slice the apples and put into a pie dish or small roasting tin. Mix in the sugar, lemon juice and ground cloves and dot with the butter.

Roll out the pastry to fit the dish and press on to the edges of the dish which should be moistened with water. Brush the pastry with the beaten egg and sprinkle with the sugar. Pierce the pastry in one or two places with a sharp knife.

Bake in a preheated oven 190°C (375°F) Gas 5 for 30–40 minutes or until the top of the pastry is golden.

Serves 6, but the recipe can be increased depending upon the size of your roasting tin. A very large roasting tin can take double the quantity easily and the cooking time will not be appreciably longer.

18
Drinks

Rosy Rosé
Somerset Cider Cup
Lime Rum Punch
Sangria
Punch with a Punch
Iced Coffee
Hannah's Chocolate-chip Milk Shake

Rosy Rosé

350g (12 oz) raspberries
3 large bananas, peeled and diced
1 medium pineapple, peeled and finely chopped
2 × 1 litre (1¾ pt) bottles rosé wine
1 litre (1¾ pt) bottle lemonade
Ice cubes

Mix the fruit and wine together, cover and chill overnight. Just before serving, add the lemonade and float in some ice cubes.

Serves 24, but the recipe can be easily reduced.

Somerset Cider Cup

Generous handful of fresh mint leaves
2 litres (3½ pt) dry cider
600 ml (1 pt) canned pineapple juice
1 litre (1¾ pt) ginger ale

Chop the mint leaves finely with a pair of kitchen scissors, then mix them into the cider and stir in the pineapple juice. Chill in the refrigerator for several hours. At the same time chill the unopened ginger ale. Just before serving, stir the ginger ale into the cider.

Serves 12, but the recipe can be increased.

Lime Rum Punch

100 g (4 oz) granulated sugar
Juice and finely grated zest of 3 limes

570 ml (1 pt) Jamaica rum
3 drops Angostura bitters
¼ cucumber, washed and finely sliced
300 ml (½ pt) soda water

Put the sugar into a small saucepan and add 5 tbsp water.
Stir thoroughly, then bring to the boil. Leave to cool.

Put the lime juice, grated zest, rum and Angostura
bitters into a large jug or punch bowl and stir in the sugar
syrup. Float the cucumber slices on top and chill the
punch in the refrigerator. Just before serving, stir in the
soda water.

Serves 8–10, makes about 1.1 litre (2 pt), but if you
have a large enough punch bowl, the quantities may be
increased.

Sangria

Juice of 6 lemons
Juice of 3 oranges
100–150 g (4–5 oz) granulated sugar
2 bottles red wine
½ litre (¾ pt) soda water
Crushed ice

Mix the fruit juices and sugar together and stir until the
sugar is dissolved. Add the wine and chill for 2–3 hours.
Just before serving, add the soda water and ice.

Serves about 20, but the recipe can be increased.

Punch with a Punch

1 lemon, very thinly sliced
2 tbsp brandy
2 heaped tbsp canned crushed pineapple, drained
75 g (3 oz) caster sugar

200 ml (⅓ pt) weak tea, strained and cooled
3 tbsp Bacardi rum
3 tbsp dark rum
2 tbsp apricot brandy
½ bottle dry white wine
60 ml (2 fl oz) lemonade
120 ml (4 fl oz) soda water
Ice cubes

Put the lemon in a small bowl, cover with the brandy, then seal tightly with cling film or foil. Leave in the refrigerator for 12 hours, shaking the bowl occasionally.

Transfer the lemon and brandy mixture to a jug or punch bowl and add the pineapple, sugar, tea, rums, apricot brandy and the white wine. Stir thoroughly until the sugar is completely dissolved. Cover and refrigerate until required. Pour in the lemonade and soda water just before serving. To serve, place a few ice cubes in each glass and pour the punch over them.

Serves 10, but the recipe can be increased.

Iced Coffee

1 litre (1¾ pt) strong coffee, cooled
Ice cubes
150 ml (¼ pt) whipping cream, whipped
1 × 150 g (2 oz) bar dessert chocolate, grated
Sugar (optional)

Keep the coffee and six tall glasses in the refrigerator. When the coffee is required, half fill the glasses with ice cubes, pour in the coffee, add sugar to taste if desired, and top with the whipped cream and grated chocolate.

Serves 6, but the recipe can be increased.

Hannah's Chocolate-chip Milk Shake

Serve this milk shake in wine glasses to make the children feel happier.

   75 g (3 oz) plain dessert chocolate
   450 ml (¾ pt) milk
   6 ice cubes

Break up the chocolate into small pieces. Put the milk and the ice cubes into the liquidizer goblet, switch on the motor and gradually add the chocolate until it is broken into tiny chips. Pour out immediately.

   If the shake is left to stand the chocolate sinks to the bottom, so a spoon should be provided.

Serves 3, but the recipe can be increased (although you will have to liquidize each batch separately).

Note: You can add vanilla ice cream to the milk shake but this may make it too sickly as a drink to go with a barbecue.

Index

All-purpose Barbecue Sauce, 133–4
Almond, Sesame Seed and Carrot Noodles, 178–9
Aloo Kebabs, 122–3
American Blue Cheese Dressing, 159
Anchovy Butter, 151–2
Andalusian Steak with Tomatoes Xeres, 110–11
Apple Pie, 209
Apple Sauce, 90–1, 133
Apricot Stuffing, 79
Aubergines
    Battered Sliced, 115–16
    Easy Baked with Fondue Sauce, 99–100
    Prawn and Chicken Stuffed, 97
    Salad, 168

Bacon-rolled Sausages, 77
Baked Beans, 181
Baklava, 205–6
Bananas
    Chocolate-stuffed with Crème de Cacao, 97–8
    with Honey, 98
Barbecue
    Accessories, 21–3
    Cleaning, 23
    Fire, the, 19–21
    Lighting the, 17–19
Barbecue, types of
    Brazier, 13
    Calor-gas-operated, 15
    Do-it-yourself, 11
    Electric, 15–16
    Hibachi, 12–13

Kettle, 14
Lidded, 16
Picnic, 12
Battered Sliced Aubergines, 115–16
Bavarian Red Cabbage, 182
Bean Soup, 191
Beans and Mushrooms with Garlic, 179
Beansprout Salad, 165–6
Béarnaise Sauce, 138–9
Beef
    Andalusian Steak with Tomatoes Xeres, 110–11
    Brochettes, 124–5
    Cheese, Beef and Pickle Burgers, 81
    Grilling guide, 73
    Hopi Chile Rolls, 112–13
    Korean Sliced, 83
    Mini Roasts, 85
    Sausage and Beef Burgers, 110
Beetroot Soup, 193–4
Berry Crumble, 200
Brandied Five-Fruit Kebabs, 122
Brochettes de Boeuf, 124–5
Brochettes, Seafood, 125
Burgers
    Beef and Sausage, 110
    Beef, Cheese and Pickle, 81
    Cooking methods, 39–40
    Grilling guide, 73
    Nutburgers, 109
Butters, Savoury, 151–6

Caper Butter, 153–4
Cheese
    Foil-baked Stuffed Edam, 103–4

Ham and Cheese Roll-ups with Green Mayonnaise, 115
Chicken
  Grapefruit, and Chicken Kebabs, 127–8
  Green Pepper and Chicken Kebabs, 127
  Grilling guide, 74
  Pieces, 41–2
  Prawn and Chicken Stuffed Aubergine, 97
  Roast Herby, 90
  Soup, 189–90
  Spit-roast, with Rhubarb Sauce, 91–2
  Tandoori, 82–3
  Texas Hotsup Drumsticks, 100
Chilli Sauce, 134–5
Chinatown Soup, 189
Chip Kebabs, 126
Chocolate
  Milk Shake, 216
  Sauce, 203–4
  Stuffed Bananas with Crème de Cacao, 97–8
Chops, 40–1
Cider Cup, 213
Coals, cooking in the, 30–3
Coffee, Iced, 215
Cold Spanish Sauce, 143–4
Coleslaw, 171
Corn on the Cob, Foil-baked, 102
Corn Fritters, 182–3
Courgettes with Fresh Herbs, 180–1
Crêpes Suzettes, 116–17
Crispy Spanish Rolls, 75
Croûtons, 195
Cucumber Salad, 170
Cucumber Soup, Iced, 193
Curried Mayonnaise Dip, 145
Curried Seafood Cocktail, 139–40
Curry Soup, 194

Deep-dish Apple Pie, 209
Dessert recipes, 199–209

Dinner menus
  American, 59
  British, 49, 53
  Burger and Salads, 51–2
  Chicken, 56
  Chinese, 65
  Country, 50
  Delicate, 54
  Duck, 55
  French Provençal, 57
  German, 48
  Indian, 61
  Japanese, 64
  Kebab Meal, 69–70
  Mexican, 66
  Middle Eastern, 62–3
  Pork, 58
  Practice, 47
  Romantic, 67–8
  Vegetarian, 60
Dips
  Cold Spanish Sauce, 143–4
  Curried Mayonnaise, 145
  Guacamole, 143
  Horseradish, 146
  Instant Shrimp, 147
  Louisiana Seafood, 147–8
  Mustard Curd, 144
  Raita, 146–7
  Tequila, 145–6
Dolmades, 186
Dough recipe, 112–13
Dressings
  American Blue Cheese, 159
  French, 161–2
  Mayonnaise, 159–60
  Onion and Tarragon, 160
  Slimmer's, 162
  Thousand Island, 162
  See also Dips *and* Sauces
Drinks recipes, 213–16
Duchesse Potatoes, 177–8
Duck
  Grilling guide, 74
  Spit-roast with Deep South Sauce, 89

Easy-baked Aubergines with Fondue Sauce, 99–100
Egg Fried Rice, 184–5
Egg and Onion Butter, 152
Edam Cheese, Stuffed and Foil-baked, 103–4
Emerald Salad, 165

Fish
   Cooking method, 42
   Marinade for, 135
   See also individual headings,
      Lobster, Seafood, *etc*
Flavoured Butters, 151–6
Foil cookery, 30–3, 97–105
Fondue Sauce, 99–100
French Dressing, 161–2
Fresh Berry Crumble, 200
Fried Egg Rice, 184–5
Fritters, Corn, 182–3
Frizzled Vegetables, 114–15
Fruit
   Cooking method, 42–3
   Crumble, 200
   Kebabs, 122
   Roasted peanut and Fruit Salad with Orange Dressing, 166
   See also individual headings,
      Apple, Bananas, *etc*
Frying, 33–4, 109–17

Gammon
   Chicken, Gammon, and Grapefruit Kebabs, 127–8
   Green Pepper and Gammon Kebabs with Tomato and Honey Sauce, 121
Garlic Beans and Mushrooms, 179
Garlic Bread, Foil-baked, 104
Garlic Butter, 155
Garlic Sauce, 137
Gazpacho, 194–5
Glazed Sweet Potatoes, 180
Grapefruit, Chicken and Gammon Kebabs, 127–8
Green Mayonnaise, 160

Green Peppers
   Chicken and Green Pepper Kebabs, 127
   Gammon and Green Pepper Kebabs, 121
Grid roasting, 26–7
Grilling
   Guide for, 73–4
   Lobster, 83–4
   Methods, 25–6
   Mini Roasts, 85
   Recipes for, 74–85
   Salmon Steaks, 84
Guacamole, 143
Gulabjamun, 206–7

Ham and Cheese Roll-ups with Green Mayonnaise, 115
Hannah's Chocolate-chip Milk Shake, 216
Hollandaise Sauce, 137–8
Homely Baked Beans, 181
Honey Bananas, 98
Hopi Chile Rolls, 112
Horseradish butter, 153
Horseradish Dip, 146
Hot Barbecue Sauce, 139
Hovis Turkey Loaves, 78
Hungarian Lamb Chops, 101–2

Iced Coffee, 215
Instant Shrimp Dip, 147

Jacket Potatoes, 104–5

Kebab
   Grilling guide, 73
   Recipes, 121–30
Keftedhes Aya Naba, 112
Kidney Kebabs, 126
Kofta, 109
Korean Sliced Beef, 83

Lamb
   Grilling guide, 73
   Hopi Chile Rolls, 112
   Hungarian Lamb Chops, 101–2

Keftedhes Aya Naba, 112
Lamb Chop Medley, 75–6
Middle Eastern Kofta, 109–10
Roast Leg of Lamb Nogal, 92–3
Triple Chops en Papillote, 101
Lemon-marinaded Sausages, 114
Lemon Mousse, 201–2
Lemon Sole with Miso Paste, 81–2
Lettuce Soup, 192
Lime Rum Punch, 213–14
Limes with Sliced Fresh Mango, 208
Lobster
  Grilled, 83–4
  Tails with Sesame Seeds, 74–5
Louisiana Seafood Dip, 147–8

Maître d'Hôtel Butter, 152–3
Malaysian Satay in Peanut Sauce, 128–9
Mango, Sliced Fresh with Limes, 208
Marinading, 24–5, 135
Matsutake Soup, 189
Mayonnaise, 159–60
Melon Basket, 204
Menus, Dinner, 47–70
Mexiburgers, 76
Middle Eastern Kofta, 109–10
Milk Shake, 216
Mini Roasts, 85
Mousse, Lemon, 201–2
Mushroom Butter, 154–5
Mushroom Salad, 167–8
Mushrooms and Beans with Garlic, 179
Mustard Butter, 151
Mustard Curd, 144

Nan, 136–7
Noodles, Almond, Sesame Seed and Carrot, 178–9
Nutburgers, 109

Onion and Tarragon Soured-Cream Dressing, 160–1

Orange Butter, 155–6
Oranges, Sliced in Ginger Syrup, 207–8
Oriental Salad, 165–6

Pasta Salad, 172–3
Peaches with Grand Marnier Flambé, 113
Peanut Sauce, 128–9
Pie, Apple, 209
Pilau, 185
Pineapple Rings with Kirsch, 208–9
Pork
  Chops with Apricot Stuffing, 79
  Chops in Cider and Clove Butter, 77
  Grilling guide, 73
  Spit-roast with Apple Sauce, 90–1
Potatoes
  Duchesse, 177–8
  Jacket, 104–5
  Kebabs, 122–3, 126
Prawn Butter, 154
Prawn and Chicken Stuffed Aubergines, 97
Profiteroles with Chocolate Sauce, 203
Punch
  Lime Rum, 213–14
  with a Punch, 214
Punjabi Curry Soup, 194

Quickly Made Barbecue Sauce, 134

Raita, 146–7
Raspberries with Strawberry Sauce, 205
Red Cabbage, Bavarian, 182
Rhubarb Sauce, 91–2
Rice
  Cooking methods, 183–4
  Egg Fried, 184–5
  Saffron, 184

Sultana and Rice Salad, 169
Vegetable Pilau, 185
Roast Herby Chicken, 90
Roast Leg of Lamb Nogal, 92–3
Roasting methods
on the grid, 26–7
on the spit, 28–30
Rolled Escalopes of Veal with
Almonds and Cinzano
Bianco, 98–9
Rosy Rosé, 213
Rumtopf, 199

Saffron Rice, 184
Salad Dressings, 159–62
Salads
Aubergine, 168
Avocado and Egg, 169–70
Coleslaw, 171
Emerald, 165
Fresh Spinach with Sesame
Dressing, 172
Fruit and Roasted Peanuts with
Orange Dressing, 166
Kebabs, 171–2
Marinated Cucumber, 170
Mushroom, 167–8
Oriental, 165–6
Rice and Sultana, 169
Tomato, 167
Waldorf, 167

Salmon Steaks, Grilled, 84
Sangria, 214
Sauces
All-Purpose Barbecue, 133–4
Apple, 90–1, 133
Béarnaise, 138–9
Chilli, 134–5
Chocolate, 203–4
Fondue, 99–100
Garlic, 137
Hollandaise, 137–8
Hot Barbecue, 139
Peanut, 128–9
Quickly Made Barbecue, 134

Rhubarb, 91–2
Sorrel, 80
Tomato and Honey, 121
Tomato, Garlic and Parsley, 111
See also Dips *and* Dressings
Sausages
Cooking methods, 36–7
Grilling guide, 74
Lemon-marinaded, 114
Rolled in Bacon, 77
Savoury Butters, 151–6
Seafood
Brochettes, 125
Cocktail, Curried, 139–40
Dip, 147–8
Shrimp Dip, 147
Skewer cookery, 34–5, 121–30
Slimmer's French Dressing, 162
Somerset Cider Cup, 213
Sorrel Sauce, 80
Soups
Beetroot, 193–4
Chinatown, 189–90
Cream of Tomato, 191
Gazpacho, 194–5
Iced Cucumber, 193
Lettuce, 192
Matsutake, 189
Punjabi, 194
Smooth Spinach, 190–1
Three-Bean, 191
Spanish Sauce Dip, 143–4
Spinach
Crispy Rolls, 75
Salad, 172
Soup, 190–1
Spit roasting, 28–30, 89–93
Steaks, 37–8
Grilling guide, 73
Strawberry Syllabub, 200–1
Stuffing, Apricot, 79
Sweet Potatoes, 180
Syllabub, Strawberry, 200–1

Tandoori Chicken, 82–3
Taos Kebabs, 123–4

Tart, Treacle, 202–3
Tenderizing, 24–5
Tequila Dip, 145–6
Teryaki Marinade for Fish, 135
Texan Hotsup Drumsticks, 100
Thousand Island Dressing, 162
Tomatoes
  Garlic, Tomato and Parsley
    Sauce, 111
  Honey and Tomato Sauce, 121
  Salad, 167
  Soup, 191
  Whole, Foil-baked, 103
Tortillas, 135–6
Treacle Tart, 202–3
Triple Lamb Chops en Papillote,
  101

Trout with Sorrel Sauce, 80–1
Turkey Loaves, 78
  Grilling guide, 74

Veal, Rolled Escalopes with
    Almonds and Cinzano
    Bianco, 98–9
Vegetables
  Cooking Methods, 42–3
  Frizzled, 114–15
  Kebabs, 129–30
  Pilau, 185
  See also individual headings,
      Aubergines, Courgettes, *etc*

Waldorf Salad, 167
Walnut Butter, 153

Cookery handbooks now available in Panther Books

L D Michaels
The Complete Book of Pressure Cooking £1.95 ☐

Cecilia Norman
Pancakes & Pizzas 95p ☐
Microwave Cookery Course £1.95 ☐
The Pie and Pastry Cookbook £2.50 ☐
Barbecue Cookery £1.50 ☐

Franny Singer
The Slow Crock Cookbook £1.95 ☐

Janet Walker
Vegetarian Cookery £1.50 ☐

Pamela Westland
Bean Feast £1.95 ☐
The Complete Grill Cookbook £1.50 ☐
High-Fibre Vegetarian Cookery £1.95 ☐

Marika Hanbury Tenison
Deep-Freeze Cookery £1.95 ☐
Cooking with Vegetables £1.95 ☐

Sheila Howarth
Grow, Freeze and Cook £1.50 ☐

Jennifer Stone
The Alcoholic Cookbook £1.25 ☐

Beryl Wood
Let's Preserve It £1.50 ☐

Barbara Griggs
Baby's Cookbook £1.95 ☐

Wendy Craig
Busy Mum's Cookbook £1.95 ☐

Carolyn Heal and Michael Allsop
Cooking with Spices £2.95 ☐

To order direct from the publisher just tick the titles you want
and fill in the order form.

All these books are available at your local bookshop or newsagent, or can be ordered direct from the publisher.

To order direct from the publisher just tick the titles you want and fill in the form below.

Name _____

Address _____

_____

Send to:
Panther Cash Sales
PO Box 11, Falmouth, Cornwall TR10 9EN.

Please enclose remittance to the value of the cover price plus:

UK 45p for the first book, 20p for the second book plus 14p per copy for each additional book ordered to a maximum charge of £1.63.

BFPO and Eire 45p for the first book, 20p for the second book plus 14p per copy for the next 7 books, thereafter 8p per book.

Overseas 75p for the first book and 21p for each additional book.

Panther Books reserve the right to show new retail prices on covers, which may differ from those previously advertised in the text or elsewhere.